Dedalus Europe 2010
General Editor: Mike Mitchell

Hidden
Lives

D1341635

Sylvie Germain

Hidden
Lives

Translated by Mike Mitchell

700039172205

Dedalus has received support for this book from the French Ministry of Foreign Affairs, as part of the Burgess programme run by the Cultural Department of the French Embassy in London, the French Ministry of Culture in Paris and Arts Council England in London.

Published in the UK by Dedalus Limited
24-26, St Judith's Lane, Sawtry, Cambs, PE28 5XE
email: info@dedalusbooks.com
www.dedalusbooks.com

ISBN 978 1 903517 92 5

Dedalus is distributed in the USA by SCB Distributors,
15608 South New Century Drive, Gardena, CA 90248
email: info@scbdistributors.com   www.scbdistributors.com

Dedalus is distributed in Australia by Peribo Pty Ltd.
58, Beaumont Road, Mount Kuring-gai, N.S.W 2080
email: info@peribo.com.au

First published in France in 2008
First published by Dedalus in 2010

L'Inaperçu copyright © Albin Michel S. A. - Paris 2008
Translation copyright © Mike Mitchell 2010

The right of Sylvie Germain to be identified as the author of this work and Mike Mitchell to be identified as the translator of this work has been asserted by them in accordance with the Copyright, Designs and Patents Act, 1988.

Printed in Finland by W. S. Bookwell
Typeset by Marie Lane

This book is sold subject to the condition that it shall not, by way of trade or otherwise, be lent, re-sold, hired out or otherwise circulated without the publisher's prior consent in any form of binding or cover other than that in which it is published and without a similar condition including this condition being imposed on the subsequent purchaser.

The Author

Sylvie Germain was born in Chateauroux in Central France in 1954. She read philosophy at the Sorbonne, being awarded a doctorate. From 1987 until the summer of 1993 she taught philosophy at the French School in Prague. She now lives in Angoulême.

Sylvie Germain is the author of thirteen works of fiction, eleven of which have been published by Dedalus, a study of the painter Vermeer and a religious meditation. Her work has been translated into twenty-two languages and has received worldwide acclaim. Sylvie Germain's first novel *The Book of Nights* was published in 1985. It has won five literary prizes in France as well as the TLS Scott Moncrieff Translation Prize in England. The novel's story is continued in *Night of Amber* in 1987. Her third novel *Days of Anger* won the Prix Femina in 1989. It was followed by *The Medusa Child* in 1991 and *The Weeping Woman on the Streets of Prague* in 1992, the beginning of her Prague trilogy, continued with *Infinite Possibilities* in 1993 and then *Invitation to a Journey (Eclats de sel). The Book of Tobias* saw a return to rural France and *la France profonde,* followed in 2002 by *The Song of False Lovers (Chanson des Mal-Aimants)*. Her next novel *Magnus*, was written in fragments, and creates a powerful study of the Holocaust and the long shadow it left. It won the Goncourt Lycéens Prize for the best French novel of 2005.

L'Inaperçu was published in France in 2008 and is published by Dedalus under the title of *Hidden Lives*.

The Translator

For many years an academic with a special interest in Austrian literature and culture, Mike Mitchell has been a freelance literary translator since 1995. He is one of Dedalus's editorial directors and is responsible for the Dedalus translation programme.

He has published over fifty translations from German and French, including Gustav Meyrink's five novels and *The Dedalus Book of Austrian Fantasy*. His translation of *Rosendorfer's Letters Back to Ancient China* won the 1998 Schlegel-Tieck Translation Prize after he had been shortlisted in previous years for his translations of *Stephanie* by Herbert Rosendorfer and *The Golem* by Gustav Meyrink.

His translations have been shortlisted three times for The Oxford Weidenfeld Translation Prize: *Simplicissimus* by Johann Grimmelshausen in 1999, *The Other Side* by Alfred Kubin in 2000 and *The Bells of Bruges* by Georges Rodenbach in 2008.

His biography of Gustav Meyrink: *Vivo:The Life of Gustav Meyrink* was published by Dedalus in November 2008. He has recently edited and translated *The Dedalus Meyrink Reader.*

To Annie and Serge Wellens

The Photo

Goddess, I have changed my mien,
I have taken on the sacred form
Of the golden sparrow, the pine-nut sparrow...
From one treetop to the other top,
Goddess, I fly, I glide,
From one treetop to the other stump,
Mistress, I fly and alight.

Ostyak song

1

A woman is walking quickly along the riverside path. She is leaning forward slightly to protect herself against the wind, which is blowing steadily on this December evening. She is wearing a black astrakhan coat with the collar turned up, forming a wide corolla round her head, which is bent and wrapped in a grey scarf with a mauve pattern; a pattern of flowers, indistinct, just as the woman's face is unclear and the object she is carrying clutched to her breast very blurred. Her coat, short and flared, looks like a large bell and her legs, in their black nylon stockings, like two clappers which, despite their brisk to-and-fro, produce no sound.

If you look carefully, you can see her shoulders and her back twitching with tremors as staccato as her steps. But at that hour, and in that cold, no one would think of taking a stroll along the street above the river and stopping to observe a woman passing by with the silhouette of a black bell jerking up and down.

But there is someone. Someone watching her from up in the street. It's a Father Christmas, relieving himself behind a chestnut tree. He's been on duty since the morning and he's taken a break from the department store. He's come out to have a cigarette and he's thrown the trailing end of his hat over his back and his cotton-wool beard with the thick moustache as well, so as to stop them reeking of tobacco smoke, which might put expressions of disgust on the faces of the never-ending line of kids they perch on his knee to have their photographs taken. He has allowed himself this respite before finishing his shift and the cold has made him want to pee. He's just noticed the funny silhouette trotting along down below, head bowed against the wind, her arms wrapped round a baby; at least he surmises that it must be an infant snuggling up against the woman's chest in the warmth of the fur coat. At first glance there's nothing unusual about the sight, he's seen other people hurrying along the riverside path, but there is something about the way the woman looks, something about her haste, which makes him suspect she's distraught, about her imperceptible agitation, which puts him on the alert. She's already moving away, her figure fading in the slight mist rising from the river.

Forgetting everything — his temporary job, his clown-like costume with his coat all awry, his hat pulled down to the tufts of cotton wool stuck to his eyebrows, his dorsal beard — he dashes off after the woman. He bounds down the steps to the riverside and sets off at a run, holding up the skirts of his red coat. The long tails of his hat and snowy beard flutter over his shoulder-blades like two non-matching wings. Since he's wearing felt boots, he makes no noise as he runs.

The woman, who is starting to get tired, gradually slows down, stumbling a little and getting closer to the river. She looks as if she's about to give up. The dishevelled Father Christmas can see her breathing heavily. 'She mustn't laugh, she mustn't laugh,' he keeps repeating to himself in a refrain that gets faster and faster. For there is something worse than tears and sobs, worse than cries and groans: laughter, wild, convulsive laughter, that's what he's afraid of.

He catches up with the woman, places his hand on her shoulder and says, 'Don't laugh.' She turns round with a start and looks at him, her eyes wide with surprise. 'Don't laugh...' he says again in a low voice, more in the tone of a plea than an order. His mouth is wreathed in steam when he speaks. 'I'm not laughing...' the woman stammers, wavering between astonishment and fear. She has no desire whatsoever to laugh at this clown, his nose, reddened by the cold, emitting little clouds of vapour, his hat all askew with a fluffy wig, equally askew, sticking out from under it. He certainly hasn't come chasing after her to amuse her and she is apprehensive about what will happen next. But he, embarrassed, tries to find a justification for running after her. 'Don't stay on the riverside path, the damp's unhealthy at this time of year and it's not safe in the dark, either ...' Then he points to the steps a bit farther along, inviting her to go up to the street. She doesn't speak, she simply takes his advice and lets him accompany her. She stumbles as they climb the steps and he grasps her elbow to steady her, then immediately withdraws his hand. He feels obliged to put it into words:

'Careful, the steps are slippery…' Discreetly he adjusts his headgear and hairpiece, and tightens his belt, which was dangling over his hip.

Once up in the street, the woman turns to the Christmas clown, who has turned out to be harmless, and smiles at him. Her smile is all the more charming for the relief she feels.

'You have a lovely smile,' he says, sketching one of his own.

'Thank you. Good-bye.' And off she goes, her arms still tight round the sleeping infant.

The man calls out one last question.

'By the way, the baby, is it a girl or a boy?'

She stops for a moment and, without turning round, gives a nonsensical reply: 'The baby? Er… well… neither one nor the other,' and immediately sets off again at the same vigorous pace as before. A way of telling him that their conversation has gone on long enough, he concludes, and jogs back to the store that will soon be closing for the night.

2

She hurries along, she must be back before her parents-in-law. She and the children have come to spend Christmas with them, a chore now, this family reunion under the aegis of the Holy Family. The timetable for each day is set weeks in advance. The day before yesterday was the visit to Great-Aunt Édith, whom the children privately call 'Aunt Shh!' a nickname she owes to her allergy to noise, to shouts, suffering as she does from chronic headaches. She is suspected of having had the vocal chords of her dog scraped; Palmyre is a dachshund with a beautiful reddish-brown coat whose yaps come out as nothing more than hoarse sighs.

Yesterday was the day for a stroll round town to see all the brightly lit shop windows and the street decorations, with the traditional stop at the Arc-en-ciel tea rooms for a mug of hot chocolate — 'the best in town, a marvel of creamy smoothness,' Andrée, her mother-in-law, insists on repeating. This afternoon they've gone to the pictures to see a cartoon, then for tea with their Fosquan cousins. Tomorrow is scheduled for another ceremonial tea with another branch of the extended family. She avoids most of these duty calls; her parents-in-law do not insist she accompany them, even though they disapprove of her unsociable attitude. They cannot really afford to express their disagreement with her openly for fear of provoking conflict; above all they want to keep in contact with their grandchildren and, if possible, have a lasting influence on them. And for that she is the vital go-between. She is aware of this and exploits the situation more or less tactfully, depending on her mood.

Her relationship with them is ambiguous, a mixture of vague affection, tinged at the moment with pity, but with annoyance and mistrust as well. The one she finds most irritating is Andrée. There is something both starchy and fainthearted about her way of thinking, of living, of loving and even of suffering; she does everything the way it must be done according to the proprieties, in moderation and with decorum. She is so smooth in her conformity with the social norms, she is almost without profile, a woman painted grey in grey, as bland as she is meticulous, against the background of a medium-sized provincial town.

The one she distrusts is her father-in-law, Charlam Bérynx. He has reduced his double-barrelled Christian name, inherited from his two grandfathers, Charles and Amédée, to this two-syllable word and gets everyone to call him by it, his wife, his friends, his grandchildren. Though sharing with Andrée a concern for the proprieties and respect for tradition, he is of a much more steely character, with the mind of a patriarch who is master in his own home, and as far as his grandchildren, especially the eldest, Henri, are concerned, he does all he can to try and fill the place left empty by his son. He sees himself as the grand commander of the order of the Bérynxes and treasurer-general of the financial resources and expenses of the whole of the family for, if it does have some assets, it is thanks to him who, starting out with so little, has managed to acquire, save and profitably invest money gained with pugnacity and shrewdness. For him money does have a smell — his own.

The place left vacant — a prize all the more keenly fought over for not being openly acknowledged on which the undeclared competitors keep an eagle eye. Charlam would like Henri to come and live under his roof so that he could continue his education in the best school of the town, well away from the commotion of his siblings. Above all, he would like to remove him from an upbringing lacking paternal authority. He believes one cannot carve a man out of a young boy without a father's firm hand; a woman's hand lacks the necessary vigour and know-how. He is equally afraid that, on her own, Sabine will fail to keep the shop, that Georges ran, as a going concern, even though he has to admit his daughter-in-law is a more efficient manager that his son was, and he keeps urging her to let him help. But Sabine is wary of Charlam's intrusive concern and insists on maintaining her independence, the double burden of her maternal and professional responsibilities is sufficiently heavy. As far as the home is concerned, she has found a pearl in the person of Louise-Marie Chevrier, who looks after the house and keeps an eye on the children when she's out. From lack of time to devote herself to the children, she has ended up delegating most of her family duties to Louise-Marie, who has become a substitute mother, while she plays the role of the father. She has become a female father who spends her days out of the house and her evenings taking control of her family again. Despite the fact that the children still call her Mama, she is well aware that the emotional force behind the word has largely been absorbed by Louma, the pet name they have for the housekeeper. As far as work is concerned, the assistants she selects sometimes turn out to be more of a hassle than a support.

She opens the door of the flat, which is immersed in gloom and silence. She kicks it shut with her heel and leans back against the wood for a moment, in the darkness. She is taking deep breaths, her eyes closed, a faint smile on her lips. She is the first back, safe and sound. She can't think what came over her to steal the little rug from the Galéries Clasquin, a velvety rug in pearly shades of pink, brought out by touches of crimson, of fresh green, with fringes of ivory wool. It shone with such a soft sheen in the harsh light of the store. The woven rectangle was more than just an object, a beautiful piece of décor, it was a silky glow, both cool and warm at the same time, a visual caress, a poem of peace and blissful reverie... She looked at it for a long time, then touched it with her fingertips. She felt its texture and was overwhelmed with the desire to take it away, to be able to enjoy it whenever her senses, sight or touch, demanded. An impulse that was as absurd as it was compelling.

'Oriental rug, woven by hand,' said the label stapled to the back; the price was very high. She went away, but soon her steps took her back to the long table covered with a pile of different-sized carpets. Then, with a dexterity and aplomb she didn't know she possessed, she rolled it up, quick as a flash, and hid it under her coat before wandering off, looking casual, in the direction of the exit. But the moment she was out on the pavement, she was seized with such panic it set off a fit of hiccoughs. Racked by the spasms, she crossed the road and headed for the steps leading down to the riverside path as quickly as possible: better the darkness than the neon lights and street lamps, better the path that was almost deserted at that hour than the crowds, better jettison the object of her crime in the river than be caught in possession of it. Better throw herself in the water than allow herself to be caught red-handed, to be grabbed by a security guard sent after her, to be humiliated. And the man who came up behind her without a sound, almost making her faint with fright! At least it had a positive effect, it stopped her hiccough. 'What did the clown want, anyway?' she wondered.

She switches on the light and takes her booty up to her room. She unrolls the rug on the floor to admire it one more time, she smoothes out the fringes. 'A child! The guy must have taken the bits of wool for the bobble on a baby's hat. A girl rug or a boy rug?' The misunderstanding both cheers her up and bothers her, though she couldn't say why. Did she perhaps behave arrogantly towards the poor fellow, who was only being helpful. He seemed just as bewildered as she was, embarrassed at being seen in the outfit of a seasonal children's entertainer, and his get-up all disarranged into the bargain. That would definitely have been why he told her not to laugh. There was kindness in his look and in his voice, and a certain tremulousness, somewhere between gentleness and sorrow. And the brief pressure of his hand on her elbow when she'd stumbled on the steps had felt warm… No matter, he'd still given her an incredible fright, the idiot.

No, she has no explanation for her act, the impulse to possess it. Never before had she experienced such an impetus towards an object, such a desire to possess a thing, even if only for an hour, solely for the pleasure of looking at it, of touching it. Slowly she strokes the silky surface, puts her cheek to it, feels its softness, lets its smoothness permeate her being. A moment of respite, of innocence, of childlike happiness. She straightens up, sighs and pulls off the label, tearing it into little pieces, rolls up the rug, wraps it in a towel and puts it away in the bottom of her suitcase, which she slides under her bed. She takes off her coat and headscarf, goes to the bathroom to splash some water on her face and combs her hair. She glances at herself in the mirror, coldly. 'Thief...' she mutters in a matter-of-fact voice. Her reflection displays complete indifference to this accusation reduced to a bald statement. With a shrug of the shoulders, she goes out.

3

In the dining-room the table has been laid. Odette, the home help Andrée takes on almost full time when the children are there, has seen to everything. Sabine merely brings the jug of water, a bottle of wine and the breadbasket. In the sitting-room everything is ready for the Christmas Eve ritual, which will take place in two days' time. In pride of place by the hearth is the Christmas tree, in a pot with pale yellow crêpe paper wrapped round it. It is overloaded with streamers and paper chains, glass balls, stars and gilt cherubs. The crib has been set up on the little marble table with a mirror above it. Every candle in its dark-red jar, every figure, every little lamb, every little terracotta tree has a double in the mirror. At the appointed hour the director, Charlam, will proceed to install the outrageously chubby, pink and blond Christ Child at the centre of this miniature theatre of the Nativity. It will be the second time already that the ritual has been performed in front of the photo of the *Absent One* overhanging the crib, attached to the frame of the mirror by silver threads. What is its function supposed to be? That of the invisible Father watching over his children? Of the Son warning himself as a newborn child of his coming death in the prime of life? Or, more modestly, that of a guardian angel protecting the Bérynx family? Now one, now the other, depending on the distressed imagination and the power of sublimation of each one of them. None of the three for Sabine — not that she lacks imagination, but for her the tragedy was so trivial that she finds it difficult to idealise it.

Georges crashed into a plane tree, doing sixty miles an hour. He had got into the car drunk, though not from alcohol, but from a towering rage. Marie, the only girl among their quartet of children, was in the car and he'd driven off without realising. She was in the habit of getting in the car, which was kept in the garden, when her brothers' games became too boisterous for her. Together with her doll, Angèle, she would stretch out comfortably on the back seat and indulge in one of her favourite pastimes — holding long conversations with her friend Zoé. An imaginary friend, consequently endowed with every attribute, including being a good listener and understanding the most subtle references. Since the first letter of her own Christian name, M, was around the middle of the alphabet, she had chosen the letters at either end, A and Z, for the names of her companions, the one made of plastic and the one made of nothing at all. 'We three,' she would say to herself, 'are a battalion, but I'm the boss, the one in the middle.'

She only liked her father's car, a mustard-coloured Simca Aronde, when it wasn't going, otherwise she hated it because the poor suspension quickly made her feel sick. But motionless and with no passengers, such as her brothers, constantly wriggling and squabbling, the Simca was a pleasure. She loved the calm of the interior, its indefinable yet characteristic smell composed of a mixture of leatherette, dust, vague traces of her mother's perfume, the reek of tobacco and petrol. She was so much at ease in her hideout that she often fell asleep in the middle of her interminable whisperings, leaving her dear Zoé to return quietly to the shades. And that is what must have happened that afternoon, Georges must have jumped into the car without noticing his daughter, asleep on the rear seat, and shot off at top speed. The accident happened thirty miles away, on a minor road. Marie was only to wake up much later, after hours spent on an operating table and several days in coma. Followed by months of rehabilitation. Georges died instantly; he was thirty-four.

Sabine told no one what happened immediately before Georges left the house, nor did she mention his violent haste either. By that time it was too late for the facts, anyway, and the incident that led to the tragedy showed neither Georges nor her in a very good light. It was about money or, rather, about a lottery ticket he'd bought which had turned out to be a winning ticket but which he couldn't find, even though he knew he had put it away in a particular place. He often bought lottery tickets, but had never won. This time, he claimed, he had a winning number and it was for a substantial amount. Sabine had not responded very seriously to her husband's claims, she was too used to seeing him take his vaguest projects for the finished article, his wishes for reality, his dreams for action. Since that was never the case, since his projects always crumbled before showing the least sign of completion, his wishes dissolved into thin air for lack of willpower and his dreams for being overambitious, she was left unmoved by his excitement over this umpteenth ticket, supposedly a winner but stupidly lost. Georges had extended his search, rummaged through all his papers, turned out all his trouser and jacket pockets, but in vain. Eventually, exasperated by Sabine's indifference to his concern and to force her to become involved, he had said she must be to blame, one way or another, for the disappearance of this now valuable ticket. She had become irritated in turn and this had led to a crescendo of mockery and criticism. As if the little scrap of paper had touched a raw nerve, set their tongues on fire, filled them with bile. They had exchanged arguments and insults with an unaccustomed fury, both suddenly feeling free to hurl at the other all the bitter, acrimonious thoughts that had festered for years in a corner of their mind that had never been inspected or cleared out. Tiring of the quarrel, but still incandescent with rage, Georges had left. The countdown to the disaster had started.

When death intervenes so abruptly in the normal run of time, it sets off a seismic reaction, time both freezes and becomes dislocated, everyday life seems futile, reality drained of all substance, of all plausibility, by its very excess of factuality. Despite that, we still have to wrestle with this flood of crude reality in spate, however cataleptic the state we fall into when we lose a loved one.

So during the days following the funeral, Sabine had started to sort out Georges' affairs. Her hands moved swiftly and precisely among her dead husband's things, his clothes and papers, to sort them out, keeping some, throwing others away, but she went through this funerary spring clean as if her mind were uninvolved, withdrawn, benumbed. From one of the desk drawers she had unearthed a tin where Georges had kept some relics of his childhood days: religious pictures from the time of his first communion, pictures of boxers cut out of newspapers, three ivory knucklebones and a dice, foreign coins, a horn penknife, a flat, oval pebble, grey with black veins, a watch, the glass broken, white pottery figurines from the Twelfth Night pies, a scout's badge, a yo-yo without its string and a revolver made of gold plastic, a piece of amber enclosing tiny insects, old stamps, his baptism medal, an envelope containing half a dozen picture postcards. Sabine removed them from the envelope and spread them out on the desk. They were all almost identical, photographs, with minor differences, of the village in the Basque country where Georges had spent the summer holidays with his family. On the back of each one he had noted the year and stuck a souvenir. A dried flower for the year he was six, the following summer some butterfly wings, now reduced to powder, and a four-leaf clover. Pinned to the card of his eighth year was a page torn out of a book and folded up like a concertina. Sabine unfolded it and smoothed it out. It came from a book of stories by Benjamin Rabier and showed trees immersed in water, pale blue with green and orange patches, half way up their trunks. Some mice had set sail in wooden clogs and sitting on a water lily in one corner was a frog with a mischievous expression on its face. Sabine read the text under the picture: 'But what is happening in the flooded forest? There are hundreds of little boats carrying field mice, shrews, water voles and squirrels. And all these improvised craft are shaped like clogs. What is the explanation of this mystery? Liquorice the vole has just saved the life of his brothers, all the rodents of the flooded forest.'

There were no cards for the years of the Occupation; the Bérynx family had only gone back to the area after the war. The last card, from when he was sixteen, bore a souvenir of eloquent simplicity: a woman's long, dark brown lock of hair, arranged in a spiral under a thin piece of transparent plastic carefully held in place with a frame cut out of Elastoplast. A trophy of his first love? Stolen, torn out like the page from the Benjamin Rabier book or received as a token of love from the hand of the girl? Perhaps he had given her a hair of his own in exchange and that pathetic souvenir too was quietly sinking into nostalgia and oblivion. Sabine put the jumble of objects and pictures back in the box and continued with her distressing task.

She was suddenly shaken out of her numbness by the sight of a scrap of paper, no bigger than the palm of her hand — the lottery ticket which had sown discord between them, had made her husband lose his head and then his life. It was in the exact place Georges had claimed he'd put it, only it must have slipped and got stuck to the back of the leather blotter on the desk. She pulled it off and looked at it for a long time. It gave her the feeling she was face to face with her husband's assassin and she felt like crushing the stupid scrap of paper in her fist. But her sense of reality had returned, her ability to think had reasserted itself. She put the ticket in her handbag.

Sabine contemplates the photo of Georges floating above the crib. She lights one of the candles and the portrait shimmers in the pinkish glow of the flame. There were four years between them, soon she'll catch up with him, then pass him and leave him farther and farther behind. One day she'll be old enough to be the mother of this man, later even his grandmother, who knows? For the moment she's his widow. But how many other, unofficial widows has he left behind? She's sure there's at least one, the one she thinks of as the 'Flower Girl', since she has no idea of her name. This phantom widow manifests herself four times a year in a bouquet of red and orange roses, in a large, transparent plastic wrapper, attached to the trunk of the plane tree Georges crashed into. A bouquet for each season, always the same, a splash of red. It could only be a mistress celebrating Georges's memory with these flowers, with the colours of passion, since it's neither Sabine herself nor her parents-in-law who are responsible for this expression of love in mourning.

The family believe it is she, Sabine, who goes regularly to leave this armful of flowers like a blazing cry. A salute under glass, a silent explosion, a petrified flash — that is the impression the bouquet makes on her when she drives past it on the road where the accident happened. She has said nothing to contradict this illusion, which reassures all the members of the family, she keeps her suspicions, her posthumous jealousy to herself, as she does her remorse and shame at having poured out all her resentment on him that day, mostly resulting from trivial irritations and disappointments, which she had allowed to multiply, bottled up inside her. At times she goes over and over all the grievances, all the abuse he had showered on her, looking for evidence that he no longer loved her and had, as she presumed, been unfaithful; at others she ponders the gibes and reproaches she had flung at him, weighing her own share of blame for the accident that had followed their quarrel. In the shifting light of the candle, Georges' face undergoes slight variations, his expression changing from seductive to ironic, tender, defiant, enigmatic.

He had been right, the ticket he'd bought did have the winning number and the amount was substantial. What had he intended to do with the money? Spend it with his Flower Girl? But she, Sabine, is the one who has collected it and she deposited it with a different bank from the one where she and her husband had an account. She keeps it anonymous, well away from the covetous looks and malicious gossip that such unexpected gains always arouse. No one knows she has a nest egg, she even sometimes forgets it herself. She doesn't touch it, the money is tainted with blood. Let it sleep in a safe, follow the ebb and flow of the stock market to swell or shrink for as long as it takes for the smell of death, which still permeates it, to fade.

She bends down to the little flame, lights a cigarette and goes off for a smoke on the balcony.

From the balcony she sees the Bérynx band returning. Charlam is leading the way, one hand on Henri's shoulder, the other holding Marie by the hand. Andrée is following a few yards behind, flanked by René and Hector, who seem rather excited. Drawing back into the corner, she takes one last puff on her cigarette and goes down into the sitting-room.

The boys come charging into the hall and immediately surround their mother. They have so much to tell her, they've been to see *101 Dalmatians* and René, who always wants to get everything he sees, but fortunately forgets the things just as quickly, is demanding a dog. 'A cat,' Henri retorts, never tiring of contradicting his younger brothers. 'Perhaps we could have both,' the more conciliatory Hector suggests, adding, '…and a rabbit.'

'What about you, Marie?' Andrée asks

'A flea, to bite the dog, the cat and the rabbit.'

She says it in an artless tone, but her reply immediately triggers off three strong reactions: furious from her brothers, upset from her grandmother and firmly educational from Charlam: 'Do you know that the flea that infests rodents can transmit deadly diseases such as the plague?' His question is as much informative as admonitory.

'Anyway,' René breaks in, 'Marie says anything that comes into her head. Just now she told Father Christmas she'd like to be a tree when she grows up! Then she whispered something to him, but we couldn't hear it.'

The reminder of this absurd idea immediately unites the three brothers in a fit of laughter.

'Which Father Christmas?' Sabine asks, suddenly uneasy.

'When we came out of the cinema, we walked along the Quai des Tanneurs. There are Father Christmases outside the department stores and some let you have a souvenir photo taken with them. I got one from the Father Christmas at the Galéries Clasquin. It's come out very well, look.' Andrée opens her handbag and carefully takes out the Polaroid. Sabine looks at it but can't make out much, her sight is blurred. 'That was a very good idea,' she says, forcing a smile. She feels her heart pounding at the very idea that the family could have caught her in the act of pinching the rug. She hands the photo back to Andrée, who immediately goes to place it beside the crib.

In the evening, when the children go to bed, Sabine stays with Marie for a while. 'You'd really like to be a tree later on?' she asks.

'Yes.'

'A tree's very nice but it doesn't move, you'd soon get bored.'

'There are trees that walk,' Marie objects. 'Mangroves, for example.'

'True, but they walk so slowly! And in the mud!'

'Trees have a different way of walking from us. With their branches and their roots they go up, down and outwards in ways that are impossible for humans. And then they make flowers, leaves, fruits, and they're full of birds. They haven't got time to be bored.'

'Even in winter?'

'Even in winter.'

'And how do you know that, eh?'

'It's a secret.'

'The one you told Father Christmas?'

'Oh, come on, Mummy,' Marie says in a mocking tone, 'you still believe in Father Christmas? He doesn't exist, so I couldn't tell him a secret.'

Marie has a technique of avoiding questions she's asked by employing absurd logic. Sabine kisses her daughter, puts out the bedside lamp and stands up.

'Tell me, Mummy, is it true that a flea can kill people?'

Sabine sits back down on the side of the bed. 'Some fleas can spread infections, but there need to be a lot of them and the age of epidemics of the plague is long since gone, so you've no need to worry. Go to sleep now. And dream of your trees.'

She closes the bedroom door behind her but stays in the darkness of the corridor for a moment, disturbed by Marie's worried question. Yes, she thinks, a flea is enough to spread the plague or typhus, a butterfly to set off a tornado thousands of miles from where it's fluttering about, a sneeze to start an avalanche, a lottery ticket to ruin love, a word to shoot down lightheartedness, joy, confidence at point-blank range, a momentary lapse of concentration to slaughter a life like a fly being swatted. But she hears another call, from the next bedroom. It's René, soon joined by Hector in demanding a last goodnight kiss from her.

Later, when everyone is finally asleep, Sabine goes back down to the sitting-room and, equipped with a magnifying glass, examines the Polaroid. The Father Christmas is sitting on a stool, Henri on his right, Marie on his left and, cross-legged at his feet, René and Hector. She notices that the Father Christmas, his elbow on his thigh and his forearm at a slight angle, is holding Marie's hand. It surprises her. In general Marie is very reserved with people she doesn't know. Still, Andrée is right, the photo with her four children, all for once equally cheerful, has come out very well. Sabine would like to have a copy, but she'll have to be quick because as soon as the holiday period is over, the tree stripped and removed, its needles swept up, the figures for the crib back in their box and the gleaming baby Jesus swathed in cotton wool, Andrée will stick the Polaroid in the family album for the year which is about to end. And the album, with the date 1967 inscribed in black ink, will go to join the serried ranks of its predecessors on the shelf in the library devoted to the family archives.

Through the lens she scrutinises the man's face, of which only the eyes, the nose and the cheekbones are visible. His eyes are focused on the photographer taking the picture, but at the same time they have a vacant look. It could be the man who accosted her on the riverside path, but she's not sure, she can't remember what he looked like. She replaces the photo, unsure.

5

She is walking at a slow pace along Quai des Tanneurs. She has taken the precaution of dressing differently, today she's wearing a dove-grey woollen coat and a slate-grey hat. It's a glorious morning, the sky clear, the air fresh. She stops now and then to breathe in the biting air, the smell of the cold, the water and the fumes. She looks at the long open-work frieze formed by the bare branches of the chestnut trees along the street, a lacework of broken, bristling lines, black against a background of royal blue. She thinks of Marie, of her disturbing love for trees since the accident. Does she want to become like the one the Simca smashed into, cutting off her father's life instantly and disrupting her own? The killer plane tree, indifferent to the tragedy in which it played a leading role. The impassible plane tree, still standing on the same spot where it was born and grew to maturity, and now displaying a memorial emblem — a fossilised floral flame.

But who is to blame: the tree, the exasperated driver, the lottery ticket or Sabine herself, whose only response to Georges' fury was her own irritation? She should have stopped him, tried to calm him down... Perhaps after all she ought to try to meet this woman, the Flower Girl, but she can't bring herself to do so, it would be according too much reality to something which remains uncertain, an extra burden to add to her grief.

She continues on her way. She's almost forgotten why she came to Quai des Tanneurs. Oh yes, now she remembers, the photo of her children with the Father Christmas... Oh look, there's one acting the goat outside a shop window. But that's not the one she's looking for, he's shorter than the one in the picture and has a pot belly. And there's another, he's walking round and round outside the Galeries Clasquin ringing a little bell to attract customers. You can sense he's bored. He's ringing his little bell jerkily, with no attempt at all to make it sound harmonious. She goes over and shows him the Polaroid to make sure it was here that it was taken, but before she can finish her explanation, the Father Christmas exclaims, 'Ah, Zoé and her brothers!'

'Zoé?'

Seeing her surprise, he immediately takes it back. 'Sorry, I must be mistaken, I've seen so many children these last few days.'

Sabine explains that she would like a copy of the photo, does he know if that is possible?

'I'm afraid not,' he says. 'You don't get negatives with that kind of camera. But you could get a professional photographer to photograph this picture and reproduce it that way.'

She's disappointed. A commission like that from a photographer during the festive season could well take some time and coming back during the day with the four children would mess up Andrée's plans when she's got everything firmly fixed already. She stands there, uncertain what to do.

'If you like, I could get it done,' he offers.

'Because you're a photographer as well?'

Why *as well*? What a stupid question, he thinks. Does she consider dressing up as a Father Christmas to make a few coppers a profession equal to being a photographer? Does she imagine he works full-time or half-time as Father Christmas right through the year? Is she silly or just making fun of him. He makes no comment. 'No, but I know someone who could do it quickly.' She accepts his offer and hands over the Polaroid, which he guarantees to give back to her, together with a print, in three days time.

She walks off, a little ruffled by this hitch and by the odd turn her request has taken. Her anxiety has been transferred from the man to the photo. He clearly didn't recognise her, assuming he was the person she met by the river the previous day. But at the moment she couldn't care less, all she's concerned about is getting the photo back.

The photograph! The word has stuck in her mind and it takes her back to her schooldays, to a teacher who insisted on sharing her interest in etymology with them. She digs deep into her memory. Yes, *photo* has something to do with light — and *graph*? To write? To draw? It's all Greek to her, but what does it draw with the light? A moment captured, fixed, from the flow of time, like a speck of mica in a swirl of dust. A moment: the grace of an acrobat performing an arabesque on the wire high above the abyss. She looks at the photo again and it is sucked up into the insistent Christmas carols all round her. 'Deck the hall with family photos' she sings to herself, thinking of Andrée adding it to her little shrine round the crib, a shrine to the *Absent One.* How strange that drawing with light can lead to such darkness.

He recognised her straight away from her arched eyebrows and her slightly husky voice. Also from her legs as she walked away. Very slim legs, like an adolescent's. He wonders what can be the connection between her and the four children in the photo, she looks too young to be their mother, at least not of all of them. Their aunt, perhaps? If she is a mother it will be of the baby she was carrying the previous day, crying and hurrying along the riverside... the androgynous baby... Perhaps it wasn't a baby at all, he suddenly wonders. But what, then? A puppy? A kitten? He didn't mention that they'd met the previous day for fear she'd be embarrassed to be reminded of it.

He looks at the photo again. He's relying on Robert, the photographer he works with during the Christmas period, to produce the print he's promised. It's true that at the moment he sees masses of children, of all ages, and hears first names by the dozen, but he remembers a few, here and there — the cheekiest, the funniest, the most timid, the most obnoxious, the most naive. Only fleeting memories, though. The four in the photo were accompanied by a fairly old couple, must have been their grandparents. The three boys talked a lot, bombarded him with questions, one of them said he wanted to be a Father Christmas when he grew up and that set them all talking about what they wanted to be. They ended up squabbling, so to create a diversion he turned to the girl. She was standing back and he just asked her, 'And you?' She replied, 'Later on I want to be a tree.'

It wasn't so much her reply that surprised him, children are always saying fanciful things, but the tone in which she said it, the calm, resolute tone of someone who has thought it through and knows what they are talking about. When they had arranged themselves round him for the photo, he bent down to her and whispered, 'We're already a bit on the way to being trees, look at the palms of your hands, they're veined like poplar leaves, and if you spread your fingers, they're like maple leaves, if you put them together they're those of a hazel... You'll be able to choose as you grow up.' The little girl had immediately slipped her hand into his, whispering a secret in his ear: 'I'm Zoé the tree, but don't tell anyone.'

6

Three days later he's there, outside the store. There aren't many people around, the shopping frenzy has calmed down, the great exchange of presents has already taken place. The sky is dull, the colour of greyish chalk. He's smoking while he waits, a cardboard envelope under his arm. The drowsy silence of the street is disturbed by the click-clack of high heels pounding the asphalt. She walks the same way as she talks, he thinks, in the same staccato rhythm, with the occasional offbeat pause.

At the window of the Galeries Clasquin she slows down, looks this way and that, then checks the time. He goes up to her, since she doesn't seem to have noticed him. He says hello, adding the ritual season's greetings, and declares, holding out the cardboard envelope, 'A promise kept!'

She looks him up and down, surprised. 'I wouldn't have recognised you … without your costume and your beard …'

'Once Christmas is over the Father Christmases unfrock themselves, it's the custom. Here's your Polaroid and the copy. Check that it's what you wanted.'

She gives the contents of the envelope a cursory examination and says she's happy with them. 'How much do I owe you?' she asks, starting to open her handbag.

He doesn't know, he hadn't even given it a thought, Robert hadn't asked to be paid, he'd just said, 'Look on it as my Christmas present.' So he repeats what Robert said, but there's something not quite right about the gift, however modest it is. They don't know each other and of the two of them, he's the one who's hard up. And the woman seems embarrassed, she insists on paying him for his trouble. Since they can't come to an agreement and so as not to stay stuck there on the pavement like two signposts, they start walking side by side, slowly, unsure of themselves. They suddenly feel they've become entangled in a grotesque situation in which they're both afraid of appearing discourteous, even downright rude, if they take their leave too quickly, but also if they linger too long. So they talk in order to fill out a silence that would make them feel even more awkward.

They talk in low voices, as if they were afraid of disturbing the calm of the town dozing in the mist, only exchanging brief phrases, which unravel in ellipses as they emerge. Words melt away in their mouths, struck with futility, or at least inadequacy, the moment they land on their tongues. Words disintegrate, thoughts crumble, time wavers in a parenthesis of timelessness. He walks along with his hands plunged in his pockets, she with hers wrapped round the leather handle of her bag, which she's carrying in an odd way, in front of her, under her chest. They each feel they are floundering, adrift, they don't know how to play this role with no lines, no structure, with no topic even, which they're expected to improvise. But their awkwardness has a certain sweetness, their mild unease a taste of innocence.

And now the chalky sky also begins to moulder too as it starts to drizzle. Soon there is nothing for it but to go into a café to get out of the moisture which is pricking their faces with icy needles. But once inside, sitting face to face at a marble-topped table, they are forced to abandon the pose of passive extras and take on the role of actors improvising their parts. The clink of the little spoons stirred round several times in the thimbleful of black coffee then tapped on the rim of the cup sets the tone for their conversation. Words become solid again, thoughts recover, branch out. Suddenly time starts up once more, moves at a lively pace. It is already starting to get dark when they part.

I talked too much, Sabine tells herself as she hurries home. But whose fault was it? He asked her so many questions, avoiding those she asked in return. The photograph was the starting point. With the tip of her forefinger, she introduced her children in descending order: 'There, standing on your right, is Henri, thirteen and a half, a very good pupil, too good perhaps, I mean ... too studious, too serious ... sitting on the ground, René and Hector, non-identical twins, eleven years old and, on your left, Marie, almost nine.' When he expressed his astonishment that she was the mother of children of that age, she told him that she got married at seventeen and Henri was born the following year. She was evasive about her husband, only mentioning the cause of his violent death. She didn't talk much about Marie, either, much less than her sons. Marie, her only daughter, her youngest, who's turned into a long-term torment.

No, I didn't talk too much, she decides, reassuring herself, it was he who wasn't very communicative. To justify the fact that he had nothing, or very little, to say about himself, he produced a series of negatives: no wife or partner, no children, no brothers or sisters, no parents, they died early, no house of his own, no fixed abode, no special qualifications, no no no .... But dreams, plans, wishes, she asked him, he must have some of those, everyone does or they're not really alive. He smiles his agreement, confirms that he is fully alive and immediately closes the subject by turning the conversation back to her and the children. All that she knows of him is his name, Pierre Zébreuze, and his age, thirty-two. She guessed that he juggled with different part-time jobs, instead of having a proper profession, and often moved from place to place. 'You go from town to town like an old-fashioned journeyman,' she told him. His reply had a touch of self-mockery: 'In a way, yes, I do ... but my journey has been going on for years, and I'll never complete it by qualifying as a master craftsman. I'm not aiming for mastery, mere survival is difficult enough as it is.'

'And if someone offered you a permanent job, would you accept it?'

'It all depends on the type of work, the conditions, the place ...'

So, without thinking about it, she said, 'Sales assistant in a shop selling garden equipment in Normandy. Would that suit you?'

'Selling what? Garden gnomes?'

He assumed it was an example she had chosen at random and continued in his mocking tone. She should have allowed him to remain under this misapprehension and quietly backtracked, but she was so taken with the idea that had just come to her and, perhaps, irritated by his response, that she insisted it was a serious offer. Immediately he put the ball back in her court. 'And what will you do if I accept?'

'Stick by my offer and put it to the test.'

A challenge, that's what it was, but more to herself than to this man she hardly knows. She's just dismissed one of her employees for professional misconduct and she's just clashed with another, so she needs to resolve these problems as quickly as possible, before her father-in-law gets wind of her difficulties and feels it gives him the right to intervene in her affairs. This unfrocked Father Christmas has no qualifications, no experience in that particular area, but what does it matter, he's resourceful, he's done a bit of everything, he'll be able to adapt, and then he gives the impression of being loyal, she feels she can trust him, something she rarely feels. After all, she took over running the shop without any training, thrown in at the deep end, in the middle of the tragedy, and she's come out of it pretty well. She's going to see him again tomorrow, the man she's just offered a job on impulse, the two of them have less than a day to think it over, to commit themselves or withdraw. It's urgent, in two days' time she's going home with the children.

He strolls round the streets, turning Sabine Bérynx's offer over and over in his mind. Although weary of his tortuous and solitary 'journeyman' travels, does he really want to settle down in one place, take on a long-term job, put his energies into it? There was a time when he had plans; he'd started a course, he wanted to be an architect. He'd had to give it all up half way through, and not only his studies. Having had to give up both his dreams and what constituted the reality of his life, he has lost the determination that drove him. Can it be rediscovered? 'You're a weakling, just like your father' — this comment, which was often thrown at him as a child, together with a few other murderous little comments, are stuck over his soul like a crust of dried pus. He feels inadequate, useless, and above all he knows he is capable of hurting people through clumsiness, stupidity. This woman seems driven by a will that is strong but shaky, both determined and confused, as if basically she doesn't really know what wants despite her claims.

He got it wrong about her, that evening when he saw her hurrying along the river. It wasn't a child she was keeping warm under her jacket, it would have been a doll, a Christmas present for her daughter, and she had no intention of committing suicide, as he had feared. She's a woman in a hurry, tense, that's all, pushed along by a dry, biting wind. He, by contrast, feels buffeted about by a damp, dreary, muggy breeze. There's nothing pushing him, pressing him, nothing driving him or drawing him, he's wandering in time more than in space and his wanderings are nothing more than a pointless series of wrong moves, a flight which ends in stagnation. Should he take the opportunity that presents itself of shaking himself out of his vagrant apathy?

Suddenly a voice breaks in on the irritating merry-go-round of thoughts inside his head. It's a tramp begging a coin. As he rummages round in his pocket for some small change, he has the idea of deciding his reply to Sabine Bérynx on the toss of a coin. So he takes out the biggest coin and gives it to the beggar, asking him to toss it and tell him whether it comes down heads or tails. Tails he rejects her offer, heads he accepts. The man laughs and plays along, giving the coin a good shake between his hands, muttering fanciful incantations and making a deliberate show of tossing the metal disc, temporarily invested with magical, oracular power. With a clink the coin hits the ground at their feet. The two men bend down, looking at it. 'It's the right side, is it?' the tramp asks, pocketing his reward. 'Who knows …?' the punter replies, still perplexed, despite the verdict of chance. But he feels relieved, nevertheless, the decision — pulled out of his pocket at random, hastily matured in the hands of a stranger even more hard up than him, thrown up into the air and landing flat on the asphalt — has been taken. He's going to 'face up to things'. Better a decree of chance, however capricious it might be, than a supposedly circumspect conclusion based on his own judgment.

7

Since the age of seven Marie has had one foot in the grave. That isn't a metaphor, she really does have one foot firmly in the ground, the right foot, which was cut off above the ankle. The right foot, the one that always sets off first, takes the lead, the one on which you stand on tiptoe to reach something high up, the one you put your weight on to kick a ball, or anything else, the one you jump with when playing hopscotch. It's gone, separated from the leg for which it provided a solid base, mobility, suppleness and impetus.

Thus it was that Marie entered the so-called age of reason on one leg, unbalanced, and once there she's lopsided. Trying to regain her equilibrium, she looks to her imagination for support, sometimes going too far. She stitches up reality, which she considers seriously torn, with all sorts of bits of invisible thread. Thus she imagines that her uninjured foot is going to grow all by itself and later on will get harder, thicker and then wither, whilst the other is going to stay for ever in the land of childhood, graceful, its heel round and smooth, its toes plump, like little white flowers. She is sure that from now on her missing foot, liberated from its body and from time, is living a roving life, romping about in its own way and dancing when it feels like it. She has lost the use but not the sight of it, hobbling along in her thoughts, hopping with her, around her, both by day and by night. But sometimes it seems moody and lags behind, as if it were sulking or exhausted, or simply disappears, as if to show that it is free to go where it pleases.

Unable to carry her on the surface of the Earth, this phantom foot opens the way to the world beneath, to the entrails of mud, stone and darkness — where her father's body went, because of her. For it's partly her fault that the accident happened. When her father got into the Simca, she was dozing on the back seat; he slammed the door and drove off so abruptly that she woke with a start. By the time she was fully aware of what was happening, the car was speeding along the road. She hadn't dared show that she was there because he was talking and she didn't know to whom. He was talking very loudly, in short bursts, in angry tones, punctuating his disjointed utterances with interjections and rude words. She remembers very well some of these words, which were absolutely forbidden to her and her brothers: 'Fuck off!' — 'Shit, shit, shit!' — 'Stupid bitch!'... But which woman was he talking to like that? Surely not her mother! Anyway, she wasn't there. And that was what was odd, Marie couldn't see anyone sitting next to the driver, the seat was empty, or the person in it was tiny as well as dumb. Eventually she thought, 'Well, perhaps he too has a Zoé of his own, but listen to the way he's biting her head off, she can't be a friend. I'd never shout words like that at my Zoé.'

He had gradually calmed down, but he was driving very fast, taking the bends very sharply, and she started to feel queasy. She did try to concentrate on the trees she could see out of the window going past at high speed — a real procession of tousled giants — but the feeling of sickness just got worse. So she suddenly sat up on the seat and, close to vomiting, said, 'Papa, I feel sick.' He hardly had time for an astounded 'What?' before the car made an odd movement, reeling like some lumbering, drunk animal and swerving violently. Then the Aronde stopped, once and for all, with a deafening crash.

Her father was dead, Angela, her doll, squashed flat, her right foot crushed in the bodywork, but Zoé was unharmed. She was the only one to survive intact on account of her fluid nature, her ethereal body. Thrown out of the car at the moment of the accident, Zoé didn't smash into the tree, but entered it like a dryad; she had simply changed her dwelling place. And, Marie thinks, sometimes Zoé wears her cut-off foot, like a boot, just for fun. That's one thing they have in common from now on, one foot for the two of them, each using it in her own way, Zoé out of caprice, for the look of it, Marie to venture behind the skin of things, under the ground, down to the abodes of the dead and under the bark of trees. A foot to take her somewhere else, deep into the humus, the clay, the rocks and down to the magma.

Down to the innermost depths of the globe and the magma, which she imagines as being like a gigantic, viscous red heart which is both dark and dazzlingly bright; a heart of melting, fermenting mud, plashing, whistling and booming in a muffled voice, unceasingly. A heart macerating all the residues of the bodies — mineral, vegetable, animal, human — that have sojourned on earth since the beginning. At the moment her father's body is dissolving there, a handful of shredded flesh and bones among the multitude of other substances, all reduced to a dark red must smelling of fat, fluids, sap, sweat and blood, storm and fire.

In the catechism class, where they tell all sorts of outrageous stories, they say that Christ descended into hell after his death. He descended — but by which way? And how, with his feet pierced by a large nail? She identifies hell with the magma and pictures Christ treading the shredded flesh of the whole of humanity. He treads and treads the must, wide as an ocean, dancing as he treads it, his feet dripping, the bottom of his robe crimson. When he comes back up to the land of the living, the soles of his feet are still dyed this deep red, burnt by the fire of all the fermented flesh, his footsteps ablaze in the dust, on the sand or on the water.

And that bouquet she saw on the side of the plane tree, long after the accident, what can it be but a glowing wound? Is that spray of flowers the cry, red with anger, of the invisible passenger insulted by her father? Or is it Zoé's mouth? She has so many incredible things to tell her. If she had to rely on the adults around her, Marie would never learn anything extraordinary, they have this tedious habit of taking the magic out of everything with their supposedly sensible, logical explanations, and even when they're happy to answer the questions she asks, they most often don't listen, perhaps even don't hear her. And their reactions to certain questions she comes up with are sometimes unpleasant, either bursting out laughing, as if she'd said something so stupid it was funny, or getting annoyed and giving her a lecture on the pretext that her curiosity is out of place in a child of her age. But Marie's curiosity being in perpetual motion, ranging in all directions, cannot but appear out of place and the more it roves, the more intense it becomes.

Her teacher complains that she's always trying to complicate things, when all she's doing is looking for a simple answer to a simple question, when she's looking for the precise meaning of a problem, whether in history, geometry, grammar or geography, and especially when it's a matter of discipline. She wants to understand everything, whatever it is and all the time; and to understand not only what things are like on the outside, but inside as well. Her teacher ends up calling her 'Little Miss Why' and naturally her classmates leapt on the nickname and fling it at her constantly during break or after school. But Marie has a ready tongue, a sharp, cutting tone, and she's well able to defend herself. Her forceful way of expressing herself to anyone and everyone brings her a fair number of enemies, there are a few classmates she plays with but she has no real friends. She has Zoé instead. As far as adults are concerned, she often incurs rebukes, sometimes punishments. Only recently she was almost deprived of the present she had asked her grandparents to give her for Christmas — a dictionary. No sooner had she been congratulated on such a wise and sensible choice than she said that it was so she could delve into the entrails of words and hunt out the bees buzzing around inside their bonnets. Her openness was not appreciated. Marie is looked on at best as an impertinent little girl, at worst as disturbed.

The Father Christmas at the big store the other day, he didn't make fun of her, he took her seriously and told her something that was both simple and wonderful: that we're all a bit on the way to being plants. Since then she often contemplates the fine lines criss-crossing her palms and at night, in bed, she sometimes even sniffs her hands, hoping to detect a smell of sap. She wonders why adults only become interesting when they dress up — as clowns, as Father Christmases, as circus artistes, or when they have uncertain jobs like street singers, sellers of roast chestnuts or ice cream, florists whose shop is just a kiosk, chimney sweeps, their eyes sparkling in faces black with soot, glaziers and knife-grinders endlessly chanting their trade, market stallholders and barrel-organ men with an animal, a cat, a poodle or a marmoset with a hat on.

And then there are the tramps, the most intriguing of all, for whom she feels a particular interest mixed with fear. They have nothing to sell, neither tricks nor feats of magic, strength nor skill, neither songs nor flowers nor little delicacies, neither well sharpened knives nor new windowpanes and no entertainments, nothing at all, and that's what really surprises her. They're ugly, tattered and filthy, they stink, they sleep when it's light, anywhere at all, they walk with a stoop, they shamble along, swaying, lugging shapeless packages, sometimes they vent their fury on no one at all or on anyone who happens to be passing. And then they appear to talk by themselves, the way she does to Zoé, but when they talk they shout, always angry with whoever they're talking to, like her father in the car, the day they had the accident. In return for their performance as walking scarecrows, they're given small coins now and then, like the ones that go chink-chink in the collection plate at church on Sundays. And the priests, could they be beggars as well, despite their dignified attire? Or are the tramps mad priests, without churches and without vestments, or perhaps failed artistes, clowns with naturally red noses and an involuntary waddle?

But worse than the male down-and-outs, in Marie's eyes, are the bag-ladies. She sees them much less frequently, but she finds them both fascinating and horrifying. They are the embodiment of absolute nonconformity. Men can do anything they like, or almost, from the noblest professions to the hardest labour, live holy or debauched lives, go on adventurous voyages. They have the right to fight, to spit on the ground, to smoke cigars, to wee-wee standing up and without having to hide, to be altar boys, to play billiards, football and lots of other games forbidden to girls. For girls and women have a lot fewer freedoms, opportunities, people keep their eye on them, they have to watch their deportment all the time, and their language, the slightest slip and they are reminded to observe modesty, propriety. So who are these women in rags, hirsute and grubby, who don't wear stockings and sometimes not even knickers? For one day she saw one stop in the middle of the pavement and lift up her grubby skirts to her waist, showing her bare bottom. She squatted down and peed there, without further ado, like bitches with their paws apart on the ground. She had been gripped by the sight, both filled with wonder and deeply distressed by it. The woman showed no modesty whatsoever, was not bothered about the looks of others, about being mocked, judged, insulted, even about getting a kick up the backside. She calmly emptied her bladder, letting her urine spread round her feet like a yellow, foul-smelling water lily. She really did make Marie think of a large frog on some water plant. Was she going to leap up into the air to the edge of the pavement or jump up onto the roof of a car when she'd finished? So the fairy tales were true, human beings could turn into amphibians after all. She'd been with her parents that day and she'd asked them if the woman had previously been a little girl like her. 'Of course,' her father had replied, 'but perhaps not like you.' His reply had only half reassured her and she had continued to ask, wanting to know how the former little girl had become a public pisser. 'She must have had a lot of misfortunes,' her mother had suggested. 'A nutcase,' her father had declared. And now she finds these two replies disturbing since she, too, has suffered a great misfortune with the death of her father and her own amputation, and she's often called, cracked, dotty, loony or a nutcase herself.

More words whose bonnets must be teeming with bees, and with ladybirds, dragonflies, cockchafers and grasshoppers as well. Now that she has a dictionary of her own she'll be able to rummage round in the language, she'll make lists of words with their derivatives, their synonyms, homonyms and compounds. She'll unearth their roots. You can boil roots down to make excellent decoctions.

The Slide Show

And the tree says we're brothers
to the rat to the fly to the hyena to the scorpion

Serge Wellens

Night is falling, the show can begin. The audience of about ten are sitting on the terrace facing the setting sun, which casts a golden glow on their faces, as if they were wearing copper masks with glints of amber and bright red. They look like a chorus sitting quietly while they wait for their cue to go on stage and start singing. They're all smiling, apart from one woman whose brown hair is aglitter with silvery sparks. She frowns now and then and presses her fingers to her temples, as if she were afraid of losing the shimmering mask of light over her face and were constantly trying to readjust it.

As evening comes, it gets cooler. It's the beginning of autumn, the smell of the soil, the tang of the air are already changing surreptitiously. Several white sheets have been hung, at different heights, between posts in front of the garden's big elm which is about a hundred feet high and fans out at the top.

As the first notes of music consisting of a jumble of noises ring out, two peculiar birds with thin elongated feet emerge from behind the tree, in turn emitting sounds which are half way between a creak and a croak. Their wings are ridiculously small, the size of human hands in white gloves which they flutter at their shoulders, their beaks are cardboard cones dangling down to their stomachs and their plumage, made from old pieces of cloth, is of a faded blue. Each has, fixed to its back with a safety pin, a bunch of bright yellow balloons which sway to and fro over their heads like weightless eggs.

These wading birds act like a pair of idiots, to the delight of the audience. Pretending to squabble, they come forward on their quivering legs in time to a frenzied cacophony of sound while beams of light circle the tree. At a blast from a whistle, the music stops and the two birds freeze; after a moment of hesitation, they start flapping their winglets frenetically and their floating clutches of eggs bob up and down in fits and starts. Then 'Monsieur Loyal' appears in the circle of light that has just formed at the foot of the elm. He's wearing a white ski-suit which

49

is indecently tight, tennis shoes — also white — and a black bowler hat much too small for his head. He has made two black circles round his eyes and used the same stick of greasepaint to draw a broad smile on his white powdered face.

'Good evening, ladies and gentlemen,' he announces in a nasal voice, raising his hat. 'I wish you all an excellent GABUZOMEU. For those who don't know, I must tell you that this word, of unparalleled polysemic richness, can mean "birthday", "Easter", "Christmas" … and why not "Trinity Sunday", "All Saints Day" or "Kingdom Come", "engagement", "marriage", "birth" and, sometimes, "divorce". It has many other meanings as well such as "revolution", "journey", "performance", "catastrophe", "surprise", "slideshow" and, naturally, "welcome". This evening all these meanings, or almost all, have their place, but everyone should feel free to vary them in their own way, to twist them and turn them for, as everyone knows, "Why do simple when you can do complicated?"

'The celebrated Professor Shadoko, whom I had asked to come and give us his learned comments on the slideshow you are about to witness — truly it is worthy of a *son et lumière* — has been unable to come, since he is fully occupied working on his acceptance speech for the future Nobel Prize for Logic, and has sent us instead one of his most brilliant collaborators, Doctor Zagueboum, a specialist on anything, who will give us a short and edifying speech on Bérynxland. My two assistants, Zobu and Gameu, will now distribute the programmes.'

A further blast on the whistle and the music starts up again, bright and graceful this time. The acolytes rummage round under their cloaks and pull out sheets of paper folded into very basic aeroplanes, which they throw at the audience, forcing them to stand up and catch them in the air or to pick them up off the ground. Delighted by the chaos they've caused, Zobu and Gameu applaud as hard as they can with their vestigial wings, then leave, chirping, 'Happy gabuzomeu! Happy gabuzomeu!'

Once back in their seats, the audience unfold the paper bombers and smooth them out on their knees to read the programme. Aunt

Shh! forgets to massage her temples because Grelot, a small dog of indeterminate breed with a blond coat that has succeeded the late Palmyre, has taken the opportunity to slip off her knees and run after the paper aeroplanes, yapping inaudibly, his throat having suffered the same fate as that of his predecessor.

PROGRAMME

HAPPY GABUZOMEU in BÉRYNXLAND
Slideshow/Son et lumière (duration undecided)

This show will be put on for the first and last time
on 29 September 1976
at the Transitory Theatre by the Bérynx-Fosquan Cousins Company
in the garden of the Hourfeuville house
with the following dramatis personae

Zobu..M. Hector Bérynx
Gameu...M. René Bérynx
Doctor Zagueboum...M. Henri Bérynx
Monsieur Loyal dressed as a Gibi............................M. Pierre Zébreuze
etc......etc.....etc......   ?...?...?...?...?...

in the presence of:

Mesdames	*Édith Bérynx, Sabine Bérynx,*
	Louise-Marie Chevrier,
Monsieur	*Charlam Bérynx,*
Mesdames	*Madeleine et Albert Fosquan,*
et Messieurs	*Solange et Bernard Fosquan,*
Mesdemoiselles	*Marie Bérynx, Michelle Marles,*
	Denise Chelles, Émilie Fosquan

Script..All the above, at random
Projectionist...M. Sébastien Fosquan
Consumes and make-up...Mlle Michelle Marles
Pillar of the family tree.......................................Big Elm of the garden

Music (by Robert Cohen-Solal) pirated, plagiarised and broadcast with
the technical expertise of...M. Gilles Fosquan

The presenter's bizarre speech and the programme which says nothing precise about what's to come leaves certain members of the audience rather perplexed. Charlam does have the key to the jargon and he can laugh at the impertinence of his grandsons, who are the authors, directors and actors of this entertainment inspired one hundred per cent by the Shadoks. They know that he regards the Shadok cartoon series as hideous and absurd. It burst onto the television screen eight years previously and continued on its zany way for a number of years. The series was broadcast in dribs and drabs, at the rate of two minutes each evening, a dose of irritation for Charlam, a laughter-inducing drug for his grandsons.

Could it be that they're still kids, however much they've grown, while he's still an old fool, he wonders as he watches the boisterous clowns. He definitely isn't in a mood to enjoy himself this evening, but has he ever been? Having fun and making fun of things has never been to his taste. On the other hand he does have a keen sense of suspicion which has become stronger since his wife died. At the mildest assertion a 'but' will spring into his mind. A little 'but' of limitation, doubt, challenge, like a piece of grit slyly disturbing the smooth flow of his thoughts, irritating them, putting them on the alert. At the moment it's a very big 'but' making its presence felt and the laugh on his pursed lips has a sour taste. To be honest, he's furious. Furious at seeing the name of Zébreuze on the programme, alongside Georges' sons and those of his daughter, Madeleine, as if he were part of the family.

Charlam has never liked him. The first time he saw him, he thought the fellow had 'common' written all over him. He was ... how should he put it? ... a man with no clear social profile, no pedigree. Sabine had simply praised the 'solid experience' of her new recruit. Well, yes, but experience of what? Underhand, even dishonest practices? At the time Andrée had hardly paid any attention to him, but by then she didn't pay attention to anyone or anything, withdrawing more and more into a mental no man's land, where she finally disappeared. After all, what did she die of if not of terminal indifference to everything, to herself, to life? It was an affliction which had broken out after their son's death, but she must have been sickening from it long before that. She passed away meekly, without making a fuss, without the least gesture of rebellion, exhausted by disappointment, by insipidness. She had even faded so much while she was still alive that when she was dead her memory very quickly evaporated. Already Charlam only thinks of her now and then, with no particular feeling, even though he shared his daily life with her for several decades. Poor Andrée, a woman who made little impression, left only faint traces. He, however, is a man who is determined to put his mark on his world, he is still full of life, he has no thought of laying down his arms, from the vantage point of his seventy-five years he continues to look to the present and the future as if he were only twenty-five and he does not intend to let himself be consigned to the scrap heap, especially not in his own family.

Not long after that man arrived, the country was in convulsions, gangs of maniacs poured through the streets, even tearing some of them up, chanting, 'The beach is underneath the cobbles!' But the cobbles were just lumps of stone and all that was underneath them was soil; the same soil that had been there for thousands of years. How those young rioters of the spring bawled and got drunk on slogans that they thought of as poetico-revolutionary cries! The echoes of these disturbances had reached his provincial town in relatively mild form and the damage had been limited, but the blight of insolence and the canker of indiscipline had still spread insidiously, becoming stronger more or less everywhere as the years passed, even within his own family. As he grew up, Henri had been taken in by this atmosphere of excessive emancipation, and his brothers in their turn as well. They spend more time on their leisure pursuits than on their studies, find fault with everything and bandy the word 'liberty' about as if they really knew what is entailed by liberty, that burden that is much too heavy for them to have taken on, precisely because it is empty and undefined, and its volume, weight, depth are beyond the capacity of the majority of people as far as intelligence, determination, courage and imagination are concerned. Liberty is only bearable when it is marked out, supervised, on bail, otherwise it's a disaster.

As for Marie, her rebelliousness is an inborn attitude, her argumentativeness an odious habit. When adolescence arrived and she became a perpetual rebel, she should have been locked away in a boarding school with strict discipline, perhaps even in a mental institution, to separate her from her family, who for years have had to suffer more tension and conflict from her than is reasonable. But Sabine preferred to follow the ill-considered advice of this Zébreuze sticking his oar into things that were no concern of his at all and kept her daughter at home, and everyone paid the price.

For this nigger in the woodpile has wormed his way into the family. Originally employed by Sabine as a salesman, he has risen progressively and has taken on managerial and organisational responsibilities in the shop and seems to have acquitted himself pretty well, you have to grant him that, but in addition he has become involved in his boss's private life and established himself as an — illegal and illegitimate — guardian of her children. Zébreuze has exceeded the limits of his competences and of his rights, he has trespassed on the Bérynx domain. Charlam's name for him is 'the Poacher' and he detests him with the silent, determined hatred of a landowner brazenly robbed by a man who slips through his fingers.

There is another, less clear motive behind the resentment he feels for this intruder. He suspects Zébreuze of having a third position: that of Sabine's lover.

An undeclared lover, operating behind the scenes with the result that the children are living amid things unspoken, lies, shame. Shame, above all — how could sons not be mortified to know that their mother's employee sneaks into her bed, the same bed where their father used to sleep, where they were perhaps conceived? Just as well the Poacher hasn't fathered a bastard! Charlam's aversion is such that he has ended up lumping the collapse of traditional values since 1968, the Shadoks cartoons, that insult to intelligence and good taste, all his disappointments with his grandsons and his concern regarding that intermittent fury, Marie, together with Zébreuze, as if he were responsible for all the dysfunctions and all the annoyances appearing both in society and in the family.

And while he is brooding over his grievances, the other is strutting about and clowning with impunity, worse still, in common with those who ought to loathe him, despise him, reject him — Georges' sons, headed by Henri. I ask you! he fumes to himself, shooting black looks at the Gibi waddling about in front of the illuminated elm, playing the fool, just look at him hamming it up, the swindler! He feels at home, swaggering like that, thumbing his nose at me! How does he dare put on an exhibition like that, at his age?... Stupid clown!

The music comes to a halt on a discord. Henri, playing Doctor Zagueboum, enters with a sprightly step, he too disguised as a bird of the air, lower down on his feet than Gabu and Zomeu, decked out with the same winglets and, in addition, three springs representing hair on the top of his head as well as a hairy beard made up of green and blue streamers. He is holding a long wooden stick in his right winglet. Monsieur Loyal makes him an elaborate bow then withdraws a little to the side.

Doctor Zagueboum makes three bows to the audience, clears his throat noisily and finally starts to speak in a high-pitched, learned tone. 'My subject for this evening will be the State. Not the state of mind, of health or consciousness, nor the state of grace either — although all those peculiar states are involved to a greater or lesser degree — neither the state of shock nor the state of emergency any more than that of things, of repair or disrepair — although those states are likewise concerned — but the State as such, in its quality of sovereign authority. And in order to deal with this subject, I have chosen a singular, highly paradoxical state.

'Its development began in time immemorial but it is still not complete. That is why it is still continually, though discreetly active. It has not been without mistakes, mishaps and miscalculations but as my teacher, Professor Shadoko, says, "It is only by continually trying that one succeeds. Or, to put it another way, the more things go wrong, the more chance they have of succeeding."

'It therefore displays the dynamics of the beehive, but without hibernation, without a queen or a sovereign. The exercise of power there is decentralised, consisting of a system of give-and-take with complex ramifications.'

At this point the lecturer stops abruptly, clicks his fingers and shouts, 'Projectionist, please!' A beam of harsh light hits one of the sheets hanging in front of the elm, then slides across towards another, wavers and finally disappears in the foliage. Zagueboum gives a shrill whistle and shouts, pointing at one of the sheets, 'Nincompoodle! Send the diagram here.' The map of a very tangled railway network spreads across the screen. Zagueboum follows all the twists and turns with his stick at top speed, then returns to his speech:

'Now where was I? Oh, yes, the State, all the states of the State. The minuscule dimensions of its territory contain a population of phenomenal abundance. Now, the outward appearance of this territory, all wrinkled, bloated and greyish, seems very poor but it conceals limitless energy. You only have to dig or, rather, pump, to extract it. It owes its wealth, its vitality to its innumerable population which constantly establish and renew relationships in all directions between its members. Having said that, these relationships are often hit by crises of greater or lesser intensity. Over the years there are revolts, strikes or secessions and the State is shaken, its integrity and security threatened. It can also happen that the State emerges from the ordeal reinvigorated, sometimes even dazzled, as if uplifted by a blazing groundswell, but that is rarer. These exceptional cases confirm the profound insight of my mentor, Professor Shadoko, who declared, "If it hurts, it's because it's doing you good," and "You're never so well beaten as by yourself."

'The inventory of the conflicts and *coups d'État* is varied. All the more so because this State, minuscule, yet full of drive and called...'

The diagram of the railway network disappears and immediately another is projected onto the largest sheet, one of the human brain. 'A state, minuscule yet full of drive, called: brain. The problem is that some six billion examples of this State exist, each having its own history, regime, alliances, plots, insurrections, its times of peace and of war, its victories and defeats, its stimulating or disastrous revolutions.' Zagueboum pauses once more, waves his stick and the drawing of a brain spattered with little flags, like the map of a military campaign, appears on the screen.

'So each has its own history, which always begins within a federation of States of the same species: the family. Of the same species, yes, but riddled with differences which, however trifling they might be, can occasionally prove to be explosive. Look!' The brain fades to be replaced by a photograph of fantastic solar prominences.

Sylvie Germain

Sabine is only listening to Professor Zagueboum's learned discourse with half an ear. She's looking at her nephews and sons, young men playing at being kids once more, just for a while, just for one evening, among themselves. She watches her sons enjoying themselves clowning around, her sons who were so keen to cut their mother's apron strings, which didn't allow them the space they needed. Now they've all left home to study in bigger towns and in a few years' time they'll go farther away, probably, each one of them dreaming of somewhere else, of faraway places. Somewhere else where they can lead different lives, faraway places where they can breathe more freely, and she can understand them, she did the same herself all those years ago, and at a younger age than them, she was only seventeen when she fled the family home. She didn't love her parents, no more than they loved each other. Marrying young allowed her to escape their sullen world. And her parents separated not long after she left, you'd think they'd only been waiting for that to take off themselves. She hasn't had any contact with them for a long time now.

Her apron strings. Funny expression, she thinks. She hardly ever wore an apron herself; too busy with the shop and other obligations, she left the housework to Louma. She never had time to spend a quiet afternoon in the kitchen with the children when they were small, cooking something together, letting them lick out the bowl, sitting them on her lap, giving them a cuddle. No, she never had enough free time to play with her children, to make a fuss of them as would have been right and proper, even to help them with their homework. First and foremost she had to save the shop, keep the business going in order to support all five of them, to preserve their independence. However, she has to admit that the constant pressure to provide for them does not excuse her entirely, she is not of a tender, loving nature, she's lacking in imagination. She's even something of a cold fish — her beauty, which she looks after, is cold, the courtesy she displays towards everyone within the context of her work is an elegant veil over her coldness and her humour is always on the dry side. Finally, more than anything else, her memory is ice-cold. She has lots of memories, very clear ones, but they rest under a lacquered glaze, motionless and mute. Her memory is like the money Georges won on the lottery: dormant.

What does she know of her sons, to be honest? She knows their characters, their strengths and weaknesses, the tone of their voices and the sound of their steps, their likes and dislikes, the smell of their hair and the texture of their skin, she could identify each one of them with her eyes closed simply by touching their hands or listening to the sound, the rhythm of their breathing. But that is not enough to claim you know and understand everything about a person, as she found out with Georges. She thought she knew him through and through, down to the very last detail, from having met him at fifteen, married him at seventeen, from having shared his days and nights, his worries, his struggles, his joys, his plans and having brought up their four children with him over twelve years. But there was a hidden side she knew nothing about, the slow drift of his feelings, his thoughts, his desire and their change of direction. Since when had he been having an affair with his 'Flower Girl'? Was he very smitten with her? At any rate this clandestine widow keeps her lover's fidelity alive, for she continues to decorate the trunk of the plane tree regularly with roses. And herself? To what extent is she clear about herself? She knows that she lives on the surface of her memory, her awareness, her desires, her anxieties. Beneath her appearance of a determined, dynamic woman, she is drifting, slightly perturbed. So why should these three young men, the offspring of her love with Georges, be open books to her? She is unaware of their dreams as well, of their anxieties, their most intimate moments of wonderment, she has no access to the darknesses inside them, she does not hear the sound of steps making their way inside their bodies, the smell of their secrets and the texture of their fantasies are beyond her perception.

As for her daughter, Marie's closer to her than anyone and yet more violently alien, and disturbing, even if recently she has displayed a certain equilibrium. But is this calm, which appeared as abruptly as her previous outbursts, going to last or is it just a respite granted by the wild irascibility which preys on her and gnaws at her? Sabine recalls the day — one among many others — when Marie stole some firecrackers from her brothers, packed them into a bed of red balsam in the garden and set them all off, producing an immense blast and pulverising the flowers. As an excuse, she said, 'So what? Those flowers are called *impatiens,* aren't they? I took them at their word, that's all.' On the pretext of grabbing words by the scruff of the neck, she has caused a fair amount of devastation and lots of disagreements right up to the last few months.

Then there's Pierre, that Heaven-sent man who has been working with her for almost nine years, supporting her in everything, always intervening at the right moment when difficulties arose, either at work or at home. Without him she would have given up on Marie, would have ended up putting her in an institution as everyone around her, led by Charlam, was urging her to do. Pierre saved Marie from that ordeal and he also managed to establish friendly relations with the three boys, although that did take time. He is a man of great loyalty, more even than she sensed that first time they talked together in a bistro, on a rainy day. Pierre is quite simply a good man, but equally a disconcerting man who can suddenly become morose and withdrawn without the reason being clear; above all he jealously keeps his private life private. Even after all these years she knows almost nothing about him, about his younger days, about his family. When she first employed him, she got to see his identity papers and was struck by the singular names of his parents: Pacôme Zébreuze and Céleste, née Bergance. According to his birth certificate, his first name is Éphrem, Pierre is only his middle name. When she remarked on the change, he simply replied that a mistake had been made when the birth was registered, he'd never been called that at home, always Pierre. She would have liked him to talk a little about his parents with the sweet, old-fashioned Christian names but she had sensed it was useless to insist. She herself was reluctant to recall her own parents and her lonely childhood weighed down with boredom.

Pierre and herself — they had each stayed in their place, neither had tried to turn their relationship, already a double one of work and friendship, into a love affair. Anyway, she has never felt that way about him. Pierre is one of those men who inspire fraternal affection rather than love. It's strange, she says to herself, goodness hardly has any erotic attraction at all, its charm is of a different order, less obtrusive but longer lasting and, perhaps, going deeper. No, she never wanted, nor would she ever want him as a lover. Over the last few years she has had affairs with other men, always keeping them separate from both her work and her family life. But none of them measured up to Georges, to his charm that was both dazzling and irritating. Pierre, for his part, comes in a quite different, very marginal category, that of the imponderables, but Sabine isn't sure whether this is a good quality or a defect. Perhaps it's a piece of good fortune, after all, to have little weight in this world, to pass through it lightly, without attracting attention or desire; you're exposed to fewer disappointments, fewer hurts, quietly following your own road, a flat road, true, but peaceful. In place of the flamboyant Georges, she has finally managed to surround both herself and her children with two simple but solid guard-rails: Louma and Pierre.

Underneath the elm tree Doctor Zagueboum is continuing his burlesque exposition.

'The Bérynx family is a common specimen of this kind of federation, whereby the adjective 'common' does not mean 'of little value, vulgar, of low degree' but simply *one* among myriads of others. So why have I chosen it rather than any other? Because it is a topic concerning which I have valuable archive footage at my disposal and excellent informants, which is a considerable advantage, although... although 'every advantage has its drawbacks, and vice versa,' as the wise men of my country say.

'But when, and where, does a family begin?A new one is born with every new union and the shoot becomes a rootstock in its turn. Little by little the older roots sink into the darkness and dissolve in silence. However, the humus they form as they decompose continues to feed the tree in its unceasing metamorphosis, to flow into its sap, to seep into its fibres — sometimes with a stench of poison mixed, here and there, with a few whiffs of fragrance.' The orator starts to declaim in lyrical tones and with extravagant gestures. 'Poisons and fragrances, spines, nodes, flowers and fruits, epiphytes and parasites, grafts, incisions, cavities, you find a little bit of everything on a family tree.'

And, lo and behold, photographs of trees — twisted, half stripped of their bark, assailed by mistletoe, ivy, fungi — appear one after the other, in fits and starts, now on one screen, now on another.

The question of when a family starts had once been the cause of great perplexity to Marie. It was at school. During her first year of English the teacher had given out sheets of paper showing a very schematic tree with a double trunk and some branches with blank rectangles instead of leaves and fruit. The exercise was to fill in the boxes with the English words for various members of the family, which the pupils had just learnt. The family tree had been made to include four generations, no more. A handful of little roots had been sketched in at the foot of the

63

tree, just enough to show that a plant does not sit on the ground like a statue. But, Marie thought, with tiny rootlets like that a tree wouldn't be able to stay upright, it would topple over at the slightest breath of air. The one the Simca had smashed into was far more solid, the impact hadn't even shaken it. Marie had therefore started giving *the family tree* long, strong roots which were capable of reaching down into the magma, since she was still obsessed with that. Then she had sketched in some vague, ghostly silhouettes entangled in the roots and written across them in English: *my ancestors*. She added two extra boxes to the one labelled *brother*, likewise for *first cousin*, put a line through the one for *sister,* stuck two question marks in those reserved for *grandparents* on the maternal side since she'd never met them, her mother having long ago broken off relations with them, and put a cross in the one for *father.* Finally she had added a rectangle, or, rather, a slightly serrated oval to evoke the shape of a leaf, and had written in it: *my friend*, with no further details. The teacher had only been very moderately impressed by this display of imagination, pointing out that she was supposed to be completing an exercise, not drawing a strip cartoon, and had given her a fairly low mark.

My friend — she could have put the word in the plural, since at that time she had two: the steadfast Zoé and Pierre Zébreuze, her mother's assistant. He always had time for her, he was kind and he was amusing. He played her favourite game with her, looking for the bees buzzing around in the bonnets of words, and he unearthed masses of them. He was the first adult not in disguise, apart from her mother, who was worthy of her friendship, her trust and confidences. He's the only one she talks to about Zoé, and also about the accident, about her father swearing at an invisible woman; she's never said anything about that to her mother or her brothers. Pierre made no comment, asked her no questions, but two days later he told her the legend of Orpheus and his beloved, the tree-nymph Eurydice.

He knew lots of stories and he was just as good at thinking them up; that was the way he introduced another person into her imaginary universe, a little girl called Zélie of the same indeterminate age as Zoé and with similar quirks. He wrote down some of these stories on large squared paper which she kept in a cherry-red file with dividers of all the colours of the rainbow. Short tales where Zoé and Zélie, or bugs, stones, trees or simple words could play the main part. One day she told him, 'For a long time I wanted to be a tree when I grew up, but now I'd like to be a book. A tree-book with each page written by the wind, insects, the sun and the rain, birds, moonbeams. Every spring a new story would be invented, it would blossom in the summer, lose its leaves in the autumn, fade away in the winter, then it would start all over again, never ending.'

When she reached adolescence, Marie gave up all these games, lost interest in the childish stories, deserted Zoé and Zélie and stopped pouring forth her secrets, her dreams, her crazy thoughts. More and more she turned in on herself and was soon tightly wrapped round a rage that was all the more fearsome for being impotent: rage at having being amputated, at having been fitted with a prosthesis which forces her to hide her legs all the time, at being forbidden a large number of activities, games, rage at believing she is condemned never to be able to appeal to a man. She was done with the idiotic make-believe about her foot going off capering underground, trotting along all the way down to the magma, done with the puerile consolations she made up to the point of self-hypnosis, done with the fantasies about tree-books rustling with words. She did a U-turn, rejected the power of her imagination, said no to the seductive power of fables and decided to look reality in the face, coldly. Her severed foot? A bit of mangled flesh and bone, long since disintegrated, decomposed. Zoé, Zélie, Eurydice and all the various nymphs? Grotesque phantasms. Her father? Everything except an Orpheus, just a reckless driver who swore like a trooper. The trees? Permanent prisoners. She recalled some lines she'd read in a poem by Valéry, playing on the double meaning of *rame* — branch or oar — about trees 'Ceaselessly beating a sky always closed/ Vainly clad in boughs.' So what? And words? They alone had not quite lost their charm, only now she didn't look for the ones down among the roots, rather those with spines and she was good at choosing the sharpest, most poisonous.

But was she the one who chose them, or did they, the words, take hold of her? She was no longer mistress of the game, the roles had been reversed, words had assumed power and they were manipulating her, amusing themselves by looking for 'bees in her bonnet', ticks in her brain, wasps on her tongue. She couldn't stops herself saying nasty things, harsh and cutting words, making coarse remarks. They suddenly appeared in her mouth, like fireballs catapulted against her teeth and bursting out through her lips. The more it pained her, the more the words increased in vigour and malice; she was suffering from a sort of demoniac gift of tongues.

By being so unpleasant in words and equally unpleasant in looks and gestures, she drove everyone away, thus proving to herself that she was indeed not lovable, not desirable, not by anyone, starting with those closest to her, her mother and brothers, Louma and Pierre. Above all Pierre, that goody-goody guardian angel who had indulged her, keeping her in a sham fantasy world, in a state of false innocence which was nothing but inanity. Not loving herself, to the point of detestation, she no longer wanted to love or be loved. But Pierre resisted her spitefulness, he did not repulse her, he took her rebuffs, her insults. What was the love he had for her? That of a father, of a lover, an uncle, a friend? No, that of a dog, she decided. A pathetic little dog, whose patience only succeeded in irritating her even more, his fidelity in exasperating her.

There came a day when the hopeless affection of this two-legged pooch made her lose her temper violently. It was when she had her last birthday, three months ago. Before giving her his present, he talked about Hokusai, who towards the end of his life called himself 'the old man mad about painting'. There was a legend told about him that when a vase, on which he had painted a view of Mount Fuji, broke, he stuck it together and emphasised all the lines of the break with gold thread, in order to inscribe the memory of its fall on the restored vase and to heighten its beauty. Then Pierre handed her a small velvet purse. She took out a slim gold chain with flat, slightly curving links. A thin flash of pure gold to go round her ankle. To glorify her disability, to magnify her horrible prosthesis? How long, and to what point, did this moron intend to go on persecuting her with his vacuous kindness in order to force her to surrender? She examined the piece of jewellery for a moment and, without saying a word, broke it in two and threw it on the floor. 'What would Hokusai do with a break like that?' she asked him in mocking tones. He didn't reply but shrugged his shoulders, staring at her with a look she had never seen in him before, a look as hard and calm, as limpid and distant as a mirror. A look which reflected just her own face, the futility of her constant violence and the stupidity of her spitefulness. For the first time she was standing face-to-face with herself, with a young woman tightly buttoned up in her crabbed misery, insisting on saying no to everything, on blocking out life. She no longer saw him, he was bare as a mirror with an implacable clarity of reflection. She raised her hand to slap him, to break the spell cast by the mirror, but he caught her hand in the air and forced her arm back. The reflux turned the blow against herself, hitting her on the mouth. Pierre turned round and left the room without a word. She didn't call him back, didn't apologise, nor did she snigger or hurl abuse, she watched him leave and, once the door was closed, listened to him walk away.

To whom did those steps belong, echoing down the corridor and crossing the threshold, then fading along the gravel of the avenue and finally falling silent? It felt to her as if her body had split and that one part of it had detached itself, the nocturnal part, worn out with anger. Or was it the other way round, was it the enchanted part she could hear escaping, that of her childhood, which for a long time had fed on dreams, fears and raptures, before being denied, banished and humiliated? From the time of her childhood, when she lived on an equal footing with the fantastic, believed the stories of dryads, the nymphs that lived in the bodies of trees, moving with slender grace beneath the bark, singing in thin voices in the fragrance of the sap. As did Zoé, who had chosen to live in the trunk of a plane tree. Zoé, the little will-o'-the-wisp who had kept her company until adolescence, the astral friend she had dismissed haughtily, her half-sprite, half-fiend double that a slap had just ousted from the cranny where she had hidden for all those years and who, once released, immediately fled. Zoé, Zélie, pathetic infantas devoid of flesh, of any power and any future, but not of life — a clandestine life, all suppleness, cunning and surprises.

Marie picked up the two pieces of the chain and put them back in the little bag. The fury that had tormented her for years had left her, a vast silence spread inside her, all the perfidious words that were swarming around in her stomach, in her head, in her mouth, had fallen silent en masse. She felt back to normal, released. She never spoke of the scene with Pierre; her relationship with him has calmed down by now, but is more distant. Pierre, for his part, has never referred to the incident, nor mentioned the profound change in Marie's behaviour. The scene is not a secret between them kept under seal by shame or resentment, it is rather a secret each shares with themself, with an unexpected part of themself, a part lost then found, still misted over with astonishment. A secret like that, different for each of them, cannot be shared, even on their own they can scarcely manage to probe its darkness. None of those around them suspects a dispute has taken place, setting off a seismic shock in Marie, a crack in Pierre.

Doctor Zagueboum resumes his exposition: 'Where and when does a family begin? Impossible to answer that question. However, it is well known that, "If there's no solution it's because there's no problem," so everything's OK. I will limit myself to a quick run-through, in record time, of the history of the Bérynx federation and its Fosquan branch over about seventy-five years. We will journey back into the mists of time at a later date. And now I'm going to ask the projectionist to start his machine and to give it all he's got, for 'it's better to keep giving it all you've got even if nothing happens apart from the risk that something worse might happen if you didn't give it all you've got.' Gabu and Zomeu reappear, having discarded their cardboard beaks, and take up position on either side of the illuminated area. One puts a trumpet to his lips, the other is holding a pair of cymbals; each time a member of the family appears on the screen they're going to squeeze some resounding blasts from their instruments.

It's too much for Édith, she gets up and slips away quietly, clutching her voiceless dog. She retires to the ground-floor room that used to be Georges' office, where Sabine has made up a bed for her. She closes the door and the shutters, gets undressed, puts on her night-dress and stuffs some wax earplugs into her ears. She knows the nickname her great-nephews have for her, Aunt Shh!, and she finds it appropriate — much more so than those who thought it up imagine.

Yes, 'shhh...!' for the world to quieten its hubbub, for outside noise to stop, leaving a luminous silence for the only voice that mattered to her, the only laugh she had loved, the only breath that had touched her heart: those of her nephew, Georges, her sole, exclusive, forbidden love. There was thirteen years difference between them, less than that between herself and Charlam, who is seventeen years older and had very early on gone beyond his position of big brother and exercised paternal authority over her, and that much more rigorously than their father. Georges had very quickly blurred the distinctions, slipping from

the status of nephew to that of little brother, a belated arrival in her
existence as the baby of the family, then to that of spiritual son — she
had been made the child's godmother, a role she took very seriously.
At last her brother had given her a formal position and, though the
responsibility was symbolic, Édith took pride in it. But every joy has
its dark side and the young godmother had soon fallen prey to the first
pangs of jealousy: jealousy of those who lived in constant closeness
to the child, her niece Madeleine, born four years before Georges, and
above all her sister-in-law, Andrée. It was a mild form of jealousy,
Édith only suffered the torments when she went for a long time without
seeing her godson, which didn't happen very frequently, since she lived
in the same town and had managed to make it a tradition that she spent
her holidays with her brother's family. Then her part-fraternal, part-
maternal love for Georges changed its nature, taking on a discordant
tone, at once both hoarse and shrill.

This turnaround happened all at once, one afternoon, beside a river in
the Basque country, where Charlam and Andrée rented a holiday house
every summer. Georges was just sixteen at the time but he had grown so
much and developed so well that he seemed more a young man than an
adolescent. Sitting under a sunshade on the terrace, Édith had watched
him come up the path from the river bank to the house wearing just
his swimming trunks, a towel slung over his shoulder. He hadn't dried
himself, he was dripping with water and light. This scene, which was
repeated identically every afternoon, had never before disturbed Édith
in the way it did at that moment. Was it the air that was particularly
transparent that day, the dusting of gold from the light, the soft breeze
fragrant with bitter, peppery odours?
    The boy approaching the terrace, shaking his wet hair, did not come
from the river down below, he was not the son of her brother, he was
not sixteen years old. He was emerging from the rocks, the stones and
the plants, from the smell of resin and a shower of sunlight, he was
no one's son and was as old as a bee taking its first flight and as the
mountains outlining the horizon with dark blue curves. He came from
the dawn of the world, an emissary of the morning of the flesh, of the

splendour of naked skin and of desire. She could feel her heart start beating violently, not only in her chest, but in her stomach, her kidneys and lower abdomen, she no longer had a heart, but a fist that was hitting her all over her body. 'Ow!' Georges suddenly cried, stopping on the path; he'd trodden on a thorn. He began to hop and she hurried down to help him up the steps to the terrace and then pulled the spine out of his heel. She kept the spine, she made it into a relic and kept it in a locket she always wore round her neck.

That evening she hadn't been able to get to sleep, the body of the young man adorned with droplets of water and light, with the warm wind and fragrances, had kept her awake in a ferment of desire. She spent a sleepless night during which she became painfully aware of the petty, insipid nature of her own life. She was approaching thirty and was not married, she had had just a couple of minor romances which had remained innocent and led nowhere, she had no women friends, her work was of little interest and she had a family life by proxy, by grafting herself onto her brother's. Sex had never bothered her very much, to be honest she was almost totally ignorant of it, she was even unaware of her own body. Why, then, this irruption of desire, so abrupt as to take her breath away and completely out of place? Worse than out of place, shocking, disgusting… her nephew, her godson who had only just left childhood behind! But the desire that had blossomed inside her couldn't care less about the whys and wherefores, it laughed at modesty, prohibitions, laws, it demanded its due and that immediately. Eventually Édith had got up, put on her dressing gown and left her room to slip along the corridor to George's, feeling her way in the darkness. She was sweating, less because of the humidity that spread to the very depths of the night than from the fear which forced her to use every expedient caution suggested, walking on the tips of her toes, very slowly, and holding her breath. She had the impression she was weighted down and yet she felt as light as air.

The door at last, turn the handle without making any noise at all and go in just as silently. The bedroom was less dark than the corridor, a little of the first light of dawn was coming in through the slits in the shutters, spreading a vague glimmer of pale grey. Édith stood still for a while, listening to the regular breathing of the sleeper, making sure he was sleeping soundly. Her eyes had adjusted to the pearly half-light and she had located the path she must take without the risk of stumbling against a piece of furniture, on a rug or clothes dropped on the floor. There was even an apple core and an opened packet of biscuits under the bed. She made her way towards it, closer, ever closer.

There, she'd made it. Georges was sleeping on his stomach, his arms folded in an arc round his head, his forehead buried in the pillow. He'd pushed the blanket back to the foot of the bed; the concertinaed sheet came half way up his back. She lifted the sheet and removed it gently. He was stretched out like a swimmer doing the breast stroke. His back was magnificent, broad at the shoulders and chest, slim at the waist, his spine straight, his muscles firm, well defined, especially the lozenge-shaped ones in the lower back, and his buttocks rounded, slightly hollow at the sides. His buttocks were in even sharper relief because they were paler than the rest of his body, which was already tanned, and their skin seemed softer, more satiny. She looked at him without daring to touch him yet.

She bent over his head to smell his hair, the back of his neck. The odour they gave off was not entirely unknown to her, but she had never inhaled it from so close. Then she knelt down and moved her hands slowly along his body, just above the skin, to pick up its heat, not being able to feel its texture. But little by little her palms, heavy with the warmth, intoxicated with languor, brushed over his hair, his shoulders, his sides, his waist, his thighs and the back of his knees. She spread out her fingers to multiply the contacts and ran the tip of her forefinger lightly along the anal cleft, first up, then down, several times. The heat coming from this narrow cleft was more intense than from the other parts of his body. Disturbed in his profound sleep by these touches, minimal though they were, Georges shivered and turned over onto his back, his arms still thrown up round his head, his face towards the wall.

The panic which gripped Édith at this movement was followed by another emotion, equally violent yet very sweet. The boy's chest and stomach were spattered with little constellations of beauty spots of different size, some russet, others darker. She had already noticed them when he went round stripped to the waist in summer, but had never looked at them closely. The darkness in the bedroom was dissipating more and more, the pale light of daybreak was already tinged with pink. His penis was folded over, coiled up in the locks of golden brown pubic hair, like a little animal curled up in a nest of dry grass.

She ran the tips of her fingers over the fine, silky hair, gently wrapped one round her little finger and leant over once more to catch the smell from that most secret part of his body. It was completely unknown to her, but it seemed obvious, familiar, enchanting. A blurred fragrance, both bland and powerful, recalling both that of ivy and of certain pinks or geranium leaves, and of gingerbread, of melted, indeed rancid butter, quince jelly, fresh milk... all these odours one on top of the other, mingling with each other, taking over from each other.

Sight, touch, smell — only taste was missing. Delicately she brushed the creased, ochre and pale mauve skin round his penis with her lips. Then she touched it with the tip of her tongue, also the skin round his testicles, more wrinkled and purplish, dotted with stray hairs. Georges shivered again at this contact, his penis quivered too, unrolled and stretched out in the tousled hair, without growing larger. She continued to dab at his penis and scrotum with the end of her tongue, the glans emerged from the enveloping skin and the sleeper moaned. The faint moan set off a sweet, voluptuous turmoil inside Édith and, abandoning all precaution, she licked, lapped at the skin, then inserted the member, more and more swollen and stiff, in her mouth. The sleeper's breathing became more resonant, spasmodic, until it subsided in a dull groan as his body arched and a warm, sticky fluid with a sweetish taste flowed out of his penis. Before he could fully wake and realise what had happened, Édith pulled the sheet back up, whispering, 'Shh... you're asleep, asleep... it's a dream, a dream, a dream caress... you're asleep, asleep...' and slipped out of the room and back to her own as quickly as she could.

Had he been in such a deep sleep, had he really not seen anything?

The question had gone round and round in her head until the morning. During the next day Georges had not shown any sign of embarrassment at all in the presence of his aunt, he hadn't kept away from her or sought her out any more than usual. Édith had behaved in a similarly normal way, but the doubt still persisted for a long time — which of the two of them was cheating most, him or her? Which of the two had acquired a secret power over the other?

She had never slipped quietly into his bedroom again, never again allowed herself to lavish secret caresses on his sleeping body, she had restored the normal distance, a balance between affection and modesty. However, she had never forgotten, never regretted or denied the things she had dared to do that August night, indeed, she made every effort to keep the memory alive — no, not a memory but a wonderful event, a moment of grace that had become timeless, a delightful miracle, an advent! She mobilised and concentrated all her powers of memory, of her senses, her imagination to help preserve every perception, every sensation, every emotion she had felt that night. Every last detail of the bedroom, right down to the objects and clothes lying on the floor, to the apple core, the dust on the floorboards, the folds in the sheet, the greyish then pink whiteness of light in which the room was bathed remained etched on her memory with remarkable distinctness, and those of Georges' body even more powerfully. Clear in her mind was the vision of his figure, his colouring, his muscles, his beauty spots, the feel of his skin, his hair, intense the smell of his hair, his chest, his lower abdomen, intact the taste of his sperm and pure the timbre of his breathing, its low, melodious moaning, and very pure that of his final groan. From now on she would carry it inside her for ever, in the fibres of her own body, Georges' body, his youth, his orgasm.

His orgasm! She will have been the first woman to give him one. A gift granted in secret, true, but with the lavishness, the veiled wonderment of a dream. Yes, she will have been the first woman to amaze his flesh, she, the maid untouched until that day and who will die in that state. How could she not have felt the pangs of jealousy that day when Georges introduced Sabine to her and brought her into the family?

It didn't really matter who the girl was, even if she'd possessed all possible qualities and virtues, Édith's response would still have been one of immediate and permanent antipathy. But she had not shown it, what was happening was inevitable, Georges' life was following the normal course. And the children were born, four in number, that too was in the nature of things, as it was also predictable that he would leave the town to go and settle with his family in another region. Then she only saw him at family reunions. As for her great-nephews, she wasn't close to them at all, keeping her distance from Georges' children as well as Madeleine's. She didn't want to relive a pale reflection of the emotional experience she'd been through when she had stood godmother. She simply couldn't. Georges had taken up all the space.

After Georges died, Charlam had concentrated his affection on Henri, because he was the eldest and was studious, reserved. But Henri had not inherited his father's charm, there was something sombre, anxious about him, only Hector, perhaps, was a little like Georges. Sometimes he was very much like him, when he smiled, and even more so when he laughed, but that made her feel sick and she wanted to shut him up. Shh, shh!, no one is to wake the one still sleeping in the pearly shade of a bedroom, one summer's night, no one is to steal the smile of the young man asleep, no one is to disturb his peaceful breathing with a burst of laughter, no one is to disrupt the soft groan from his lips at the surge of pleasure…

Then there's Marie, for a long time a real bane on the whole family. Despite that, she's the only one Édith concerns herself with, she senses a parallel between them in excess, suffering and rebellion. Early on Édith allowed the force of her desire to end up in a cul de sac, but that is the way things are and she doesn't regret it. She blew all the daring she had in her on one episode, at Georges' bedside. Since then she has only had her dream, an interminable insomniac dream. She wonders what will become of Marie, who has at least had the courage to express her anger early on, to give vent to her pain, to expose her excesses to the light of day. She envies Marie her boldness, her impertinence, her inventiveness. The only thing she does is to take —

piously, pathetically — a surreptitious bunch of red roses to the place where Georges killed himself, one for each season of the year. She should have behaved like Marie pulverising the balsam in the garden just for fun, she should have flung herself into the real world and set fire to the fatal tree, transformed it into a torch, making its trunk burst into flames instead of into bloom. Once, when she saw the plane tree that she had just decorated with her flaming bouquet, she had had the idea of replaying the fatal moment, of copying the accident. She had accelerated, heading straight for the tree, and had squealed to a halt only a few centimetres from the trunk. Her whole body was trembling from the effect of the jolt, but not her hands firmly holding the wheel, nor her gaze staring straight ahead. Stopping at the last thing seen by Georges, Édith had immersed herself in the image, stretching out over several long minutes what had lasted only a fraction of a second at the moment of the accident.

Her feelings towards Sabine have not changed very much, her animosity has just abated with time, turning into indifference. Charlam told her his suspicions about Sabine and Zébreuze, that very handy man, but it was of no importance to her. Let the widow amuse herself with anyone she likes, she couldn't care less. In fact she'd almost welcome it, it would confirm her in the role of Georges' most faithful lover. Andrée had been eaten away with silent grief, almost to the point of extinction. Édith has more resistance, it's nearly thirty years now that she's been carrying a secret which delights her as much as it torments her.

Aunt Shh! Yes, it's a suitable name, scandalously suitable.

The succession of slides made from family photos has started. Since the evening is dedicated to Charlam, their common ancestor, the series starts with him. He sprawls across one of the screens, naked, a smile on his face and his bottom in the air, on a shag-pile rug. A photo of Andrée at the same age appears symmetrically on another sheet and the slides continue to follow one another, fast-forwarding through time, always two by two, up to the marriage of Andrée Simone Jeanne Yvette Garvelle and Charles-Amédée Georges Donat Bérynx. It strikes Sabine that there was nothing distinctive about Charlam as a child and as an adolescent, he looked banal, even insipid, it was only as he grew older that he created an imposing presence. The reverse happened with his wife, the cheerful infant, the radiant young girl had gradually faded, shrivelled; it was enough to make you think the one had nibbled away at the other, like an insatiable termite. Édith often appears in group photos, the aunt sprouting like a belated shoot in the shadow of her brother. The years have passed her by without much change, she has acquired as few wrinkles as white hairs among the brown, also as little flexibility as geniality. Georges used to claim his aunt was less stiff than she let show, that she had a passionate side that was really quite charming. Sabine wonders where the charm of this dragon-castrator of canine vocal cords can lie.

Georges and Madeleine take over on the screens, each flanked by their better halves, Sabine Dréhaut and Albert Fosquan, and they are followed until the couples are formed. Doctor Zagueboum is more and more losing control of the situation, comments come from all sides, Gabu and Zomeu make a racket at the wrong moments, the projectionist has problems with his machine, which tends to stick, and the chaos gets worse when it's the turn of the third generation. At last the band of Shadoks can give free rein to their jokes, their high spirits, their generation has burst into life. The photos of the Bérynx children alternate with those of the Fosquan boys: baptisms, first communions, holidays here and there.

It is the turn of Madeleine and Albert Fosquan to retire, too tired to stay up any longer. Sabine and Marie see them to their rooms. The house has been transformed into a hotel for the night, the Bérynx boys, having given up their beds to their guests, will sleep in an inn a couple of miles away, together with their cousins. All the while the pace of the projection is getting faster. 'When you don't know where you're going,' Doctor Zagueboum exclaims, 'you have to go there as quickly as possible!' Immediately he and his accomplices start to vie with each other in producing Shadokian maxims. Among the flood of photos one appears with the four Bérynx children grouped round a Father Christmas: Henri head up, his arms hanging down stiffly, Marie with a sparkling smile, René and Hector squatting cross-legged at the Father Christmas's feet. The reproduction is a bit pale and blurred from the enlargement, but some details stand out unexpectedly, for example the broad, flat cheekbones of the man in disguise, the lozenge shape of the ridge of his nose, that also flattened, and his stretched eyelids, his direct and yet somehow slightly volatile look. Charlam leans his head forward, knitting his brows, to examine the picture from close up. He has time to scrutinise it because it is stuck there for a moment, Sébastien having difficulty with the projector again. The man who is three-quarters hidden by his disguise is still recognisable. The boys and the man concerned, too distracted by their Shadokian game, do not pay particular attention to it. When Sabine and Marie return, the slide show is continuing, with several more fits and starts.

By the time the performance ends, the audience is very sparse. Aunt Shh!, the Fosquan parents, then Louma and, finally, Bernard and Solange with Émilie asleep in her Moses basket went off to bed one after another. Sabine, Marie and the cousins' girlfriends go to help the Shadoks put their stuff away. Charlam hasn't moved from his seat, it's as if he's soldered to it. He's ruminating. So his daughter-in-law lied, she'd recruited her 'sales assistant' off the street and not through an advert as she claimed, picked him up from the pavement like a dog-end, or a tart! And later on she'd shown no compunction about promoting him, about inviting him into the home and, finally, into her bedroom. For now he's sure, his suspicions have been confirmed — Zébreuze is her lover.

That's what she replaced Georges with! A mountebank, touting for business in the street, a common tramp with a broken nose. And who knows under what circumstances ... And that hardly eighteen months after Georges died. But who's to say they hadn't known each other longer, that pair of swindlers. He's disgusted by the very thought. Finally he gets up and sets off for Henri's room which has been put at his disposal for the night.

As he reaches the top of the stairs, he meets Zébreuze, who is about to go down after having hurried up to collect his clothes, which he had left in Henri's room where he donned his Gibi outfit. Pierre hardly has time to open his mouth to wish him good night than Charlam spits in his face and stalks off haughtily. He closes the bedroom door with a sharp clack and silence returns. Pierre stands there, frozen, on the top step, clutching the bundle of clothes to his stomach and leaning forward from the waist, as if he were looking at something at the bottom of the stairs or had been punched in the stomach. The sleeves of the white ski-suit that formed his costume as a Gibi and which he'd started to take off, are hanging down by his thighs and his mini bowler hat held on by an elastic band has slipped down over his left ear. The gob of spit on his face has paralysed him, like a large spider or a swelling full of thick pus, he can't wipe it off, can't touch it. The spit is a nail condemning him to stay put. All thought has stopped, his mind is gaping wide, empty, stuck in a pale cloud of mist. A shiver, sharp as an arrow of ice, springs up under his skull and runs down all the way to his heels. He is trembling — with cold with dizziness with surrender — his teeth clench and then start chattering. He would like to move, to shout or even weep, to escape from the grip in which this smear of saliva holds him; impossible, the spit keeps him paralysed. He feels suffocated by his inability to shout to weep to move, his breath wheezes through his teeth. He's sweating, with cold with solitude with surrender, the circles of kohl round his eyes and his painted-on smile are smudged, the spittle is becoming streaked with black.

Voices and laughter come from outside. 'And a good gabuzomeu to all' can be heard, in place of good night. Finally the doors slam, two cars start and leave slowly, the Shadoks are off to continue their celebrations at a night club before going to the inn. Sabine and Marie come back into the house without making a noise, everyone else is surely asleep and they are about to switch off the light in the hall when they see a bizarre silhouette at the top of the stairs. Monsieur Loyal is more clownish than a clown, half undressed, he's standing lopsidedly on the edge of the landing, he looks as if he has four arms, two plump white ones dangling across his thighs and two thin bare ones encircling a bundle which gives him a fat paunch. He has owl eyes and an imbecile smile, his pale face smeared with black. The two women have a fit of the giggles, which they stifle as well as they can, they twist and turn as they try to keep the laughter down as much as possible, it brings tears to their eyes. From the top of the stairs he shouts at them, 'Don't laugh! Don't laugh!' but the sound that comes from his lips is a whine as pathetic as the would-be yaps of Édith's dog Grelot.

The icy shiver that cleft his body from top to bottom has set off back in the opposite direction, licking up his legs, his spine, his neck and spreading along his arms. He drops the clothes he was clutching and starts gesticulating, as if imitating the contortions of the two women, who are still in the grip of uncontrollable laughter. He looks like a goose, plucked from head to sternum, flapping the air with his skeleton wings while their feathers, compressed into thick stalactites, slap at his sides. He almost loses his balance and comes hurtling down the stairs as if the devil were at his heels. He tears past the laughing women, opens the door and dashes out. The mother and her daughter take several minutes to calm down, finally they straighten up, completely out of breath. 'It's a long time since I've laughed so much,' Sabine says, wiping her eyes. 'What an idiot, that Pierre, what a clown!'

'Where do you think he's off to?' Marie asks, going out onto the terrace and looking round. But it's a dark night and she can't see anything. Sabine comes out to join her, calling in a low voice, 'Pierre! Pierre!…' Marie joins in: 'Cooee, Pierre!' Nothing. They go down to the avenue leading to the road, calling in all directions, first of all towards the village, then the fields, finally the copse of hornbeam and holly. All they hear are the faint noises of the foliage and nocturnal birds. And in these sounds, familiar though they are, they sense something bizarre, a vague unease — a cleft of silence. They wait a while, then, together, in the same hesitant voice, they ask the night, 'Pierre…?'

Pierre, Pierre, the name shouted out to different points of the compass suddenly sounds hollow, without force, without content. Pierre, Pierre, a porous, crumbly word which dies away as soon as it's spoken. Suddenly Zébreuze's double first name pops up in Sabine's memory, she read it one day in his papers and she calls out, 'Pierre-Éphrem?' as if with the ballast of the second word dredged up from limbo her call would have greater substance. 'Let's go in,' Marie suggests, not having caught the word her mother used, 'It's starting to drizzle.'

The Bérynx boys, their Fosquan cousins and their girlfriends leave the night club, after a long prolongation of their happy gabuzomeu, and go to their hotel. Édith has not gone to bed, she's sitting on the edge of the couch without having pulled back the sheets, her back very straight, staring straight ahead. Since she's in the habit of reading before going to sleep, she searched the bookshelves for something to glance through, but Georges was not a great reader, he quickly found novels, apart from detective stories, boring. These are not at all to Édith's taste, she didn't even bother to take one out. At the end of one of the shelves she noticed a slightly battered tin. She passed her fingers over the metal, the bumps and dents are soft to the touch. She recognised it with the tips of her fingers, it was the tin in which her mother used to keep the biscuits she made. Her mother was a poor cook but she excelled in one limited area, the making of almond biscuits, butter cracknels and orange macaroons. Édith could almost taste her mother's pride and joy in her mouth. She went to sit on the couch, placed the tin on her knees and lifted the lid slightly, dreaming of letting out a warm smell of sugar, butter, toasted almonds and orange peel. All she found was a jumble of objects and a small pile of postcards. Her disappointment didn't last long, it was almost immediately supplanted by another emotion, which grew stronger and stronger.

With her first glance into the tin she recognised part of the contents: the black-veined grey pebble with which Georges had achieved an extraordinary series of bounces skimming it across the river and which had ended up in a tuft of grass on the other side, the pesetas he used to sneak out of the tip left on the table when they went to eat in Spain, the set of ivory knucklebones his grandfather had given him. And the stamps he used to tear off the envelopes without waiting for them to be opened, and the figurines from the Twelfth Night cake that he coveted more than the cake itself and the crown... Memories came pouring back, jostling each other inside her head. She took out the objects one by one, weighing them in the palm of her hand as if they were natural pearls or gold nuggets. Then she opened the envelope and proceeded to go through the postcards. One, two, three, still an infant with petals and clover leaves stuck to the back of the pictures, or an illustration from a story by Benjamin Rabier; she read and reread the text underneath until she knew it off by heart: 'But what is happening in the flooded forest? There are hundreds of little boats carrying field mice, shrews, water voles and squirrels. And all these improvised craft are shaped like clogs. What is the explanation of this mystery? Liquorice the vole has just saved the life of his brothers, all the rodents of the flooded forest.' Four, five, the child is growing up, the war is over, flowers and clover have lost their appeal, the clamour of the outside world has burst in on the young boy, a photo of General Leclerc and General de Gaulle entering a liberated Paris has taken over from the little rodents saved by the brave mole, Liquorice, tanks are more impressive than floating clogs. Édith turned over the sixth card. She didn't understand straight away, all she saw was a black thread rolled up under a thin film of plastic. A black thread, what was that about? Did it have anything to do with Leclerc, who had died that year? But then why a thread coiled up in a spiral? She bent down to examine it more closely, knitting her brows with the effort. Suddenly she straightened up, clapping her hand to her mouth as an exclamation of astonishment erupted. The blood rushed to her face as she went bright red from forehead to neck. And the dull turmoil, the roaring in her ears that were blocked with wax plugs! Her hand dropped, inert.

So Georges knew, had always known that the orgasm that had overcome him that night had not come as if by magic, but that a woman had leant over him, had caressed him, had kissed his penis, had embraced it with her lips, her tongue, and that the woman was his aunt. He knew, he'd always known! A single one of her hairs had sufficed to mark her crime... Her what exactly? Her theft, her rape, her madness, her abduction, her violation, her obscenity, her betrayal? How should her deed be described? But afterwards Georges had not shown her the least hostility, neither disgust nor suspicion, and he had kept the hair like a talisman, testimony to a moment of joy.

He knew, then. They had shared the secret, a delicious, shameful secret, but each in their own corner. Had he spent the following nights waiting for her, had he hoped she would come back to his bedroom, would lie down alongside him, that they would be lovers? Had she disappointed his expectation? What had he thought of her? And had he confided their secret to his wife later on, and if so, how had he put it?

He knew. But did he know what she did later on — the ultimate theft, the ultimate gift? On hearing about the accident from Sabine, Charlam and Andrée had immediately got into their car to go to the hospital, and she had joined them. Georges was completely covered with a white sheet. A doctor had told them that it would be better if they did not see the body, at least not the face, it had been disfigured and the sight might be too much for them. Neither Sabine nor Charlam showed any desire to reject his advice, the doctor's embarrassment was dissuasive enough. And all the time there was Marie in the operating theatre. Andrée had asked to see not his face, but his hand, at least that, his hand. Did she need to convince herself that this aberration she was being informed of, the death of her son, was a reality? What was there to say that it really was him under the piece of cotton? She would recognise his hand, and she wanted to hold it tight in her own one last time. 'His hands have also been damaged, badly damaged,' the doctor warned her. Nevertheless Andrée had gone to the foot of the bed and had uncovered her son's feet. They had not been spared by the accident either. She turned away and left the room, shaking her head vigorously as if to say, 'no, no, no,' no to this insane story, to this brutal invisibility of her son. Édith had been left there by herself for a moment. She lifted the sheet, confronted the sight. The doctor was right, his face was unrecognisable, a pulp, his chest stove in, not a single beauty spot could be made out any more, his shoulders, knees had been dislocated, his forearms and legs torn to shreds, but the middle of his body was unscathed. Édith leant her cheek against Georges' lower abdomen, resting there for a moment, then, for the second and last time, she had kissed his penis, after which she covered him up with the sheet again. The room was bare, the smell of the place sour, the light harsh, the silence corrosive.

Do the dead know what we say and do round their bodies, she wondered, for a dead man is not a dreamer or a sleeper, he can't be tricked, can't be deluded with sweet lies, it would be futile, stupid even to whisper to him, 'You're asleep, asleep… it's a dream, a dream caress, a kiss in your dream…' No, a dead man doesn't sleep, doesn't dream, nor is he reduced to his corpse, which commands attention as an outward sign of permanent absence, of total insensibility. So what is he doing? He is in the process of transhumance, of discovery, a living being experimenting with another way of being alive, a way as unaccustomed to him as it is to those who remain on the move here on Earth, in the light of day, among familiar things. He's a living being that is in motion in another place, differently, and his thoughts make no noise at all as they scour off the rust, sharpen themselves. We mustn't hold him back, slow him down, try to seduce him to divert him from his work as a young dead being, a new living being. So Édith did not repeat the words she had whispered all those years ago close to his body benumbed with orgasmic pleasure, she didn't lie, she simply said, in a firm voice, 'You're not sleeping, you're not dreaming, you really are dead. Off you go!'

The first to have amazed his flesh, fired his senses, Édith was also the last to glorify Georges' body, to kiss his unviewable body, the body of a skinned animal whose flesh was just so much meat. The first, the last and the only one to give him her blessing with a kiss both chaste and bold, of absolute solitude.

An obscure memory surfaces and spreads round her mouth, a persistent taste of melted butter, egg yolk and brown sugar, of toasted almonds, vanilla pod and candied orange peel, of warm skin and the sperm of a young man, of his cold skin, encrusted, scrubbed with disinfectant. She ends up falling asleep on the edge of the couch, her hands in the tin of relics on her knees.

In the next room Charlam has woken up. His sleeping pill wasn't strong enough or, rather, he was too irritated by the events of the evening — that Zébreuze's everywhere, he's really dug himself into the family, clowning around like a little boy, he's intolerable. 'Pooh!' he snorts, half opening his eyes. He goes through the scene on the stairs again when he spat the Poacher in the face. I mean, going round like that, shirt all undone and sweating, in a house that isn't his! Spitting at him was quite spontaneous and he doesn't regret it, the man had been asking for it for a long time. It's done now and quite right too. He's going to have things out with that schemer today, that philandering 'Father Christmas', that gigolo 'Gibi'. And once more he asks himself: How could Sabine replace Georges with *that*! A flat-faced beanpole with a nose like a spatula and slitty eyes the colour of dishwater! He raises himself up on one elbow, lights the bedside lamp to find his tin of sleeping pills, takes half a tablet and lies down again as determined to get a few hours sleep as he is to settle his score with Zébreuze as soon as possible.

In the room across the landing breathing mingles peacefully with gurgling. Little Emily, replete from the feed her mother has just given her, is playing with her fingers. She's in her parents' bed, ensconced between their pillows, from time to time she drums her fingers on this one's head, that one's nose. She is sated with the warmth and the smell of the bodies of the two grown-ups round her as much as with the milk. A ray of light appears, quivering, before her eyes. 'Oh!' she says with a gurgling laugh, and gives up her game in order to try and catch the ray, but when it moves she gets annoyed and starts kicking her feet in the air and in no time at all she's whimpering then crying. Still fast asleep, her mother puts her hand on Emily's tummy and she calms down, closes her eyes and goes to sleep herself. Thus sleep does its rounds of the house, visiting then leaving the upstairs rooms without a sound, returning, lingering or not, as the case may be.

On the ground floor, where Sabine and Marie are camping out on the sofa in the sitting-room, sleep veers to and fro, filling the minds of the two sleepers with fragments of images and words taken from the slide show, which thus continues, but in a chaotic, jerky sequence. Under Marie's eyelids a deep well opens up. Leaning on the rim, she contemplates the disc of grey water gleaming at the bottom. She's thirsty and would like to get at the water but there's no bucket on the end of the pulley rope. At least I could throw some stones into it, she thinks. There's none of those either, all round is nothing but bare, dry earth. So she throws in some names instead of stones: 'Papa! Zagueboum! Grelot! Grandmother Andrée! Albert! Gibi! Édith! Henri! Mummy! Shadoko! Solange! Louma! René! Madeleine!…' All the names called out or mentioned during the evening's entertainment drop one by one as insults and the sound, amplified by the shaft, mineralises and each name becomes a stone which goes 'plop' as it hits the water and a face appears fleetingly in the rippled surface, but not one that corresponds to the name that has just been uttered, it's all mixed up. 'Gilles! Michelle! Charlam!…'

Each name is followed by the same dull sound. 'Hector! Sébastien! Émilie! Zomeu! Éphrem!…' There is no cavernous 'plop' echoing this last name thrown into the well, the name-stone does not plunge straight down like the others, it falls like a downy feather or a leaf, slowly and silently, and no face appears, all that happens is that the grey of the water takes on a silvery gleam. Marie leans forward, listening, eventually she hears a very faint murmur. She sighs in her sleep and turns over.

Under Sabine's eyelids it's snowing. The flakes are very light. She's squatting down trying to gather them to build a snowman, but the balls she makes crumble between her fingers and trickle out in dribbles of sand. A snowman, or sandman, appears all the same, but it's stretched out and fairly shapeless, the outline of a man lying down on the ground like the recumbent statues so worn by time that you can't tell whether it's a knight, a queen, a prince or a saint. The reclining silhouette softens, cracks appear all over the crust of snow/sand and it falls away, but there's nothing underneath, nothing but bones: femurs, ribs, shoulder-blades, ulnas, hipbones, collarbones, but no skulls, no vertebra or finger-bones. She sorts them out in groups, forming little piles. The one with the shoulder-blades collapses and the bones, which look like a long S, arrange themselves in a sinuous line with a voice commentating in a monotonous tone, 'S for Sentence, S for Sun, S for Saga, S for Saraband, S for Soprano, S for Seven, S for Salvation, S for Sabine.' There the voice seems to get stuck and repeats 'Sabine', separating the two syllables slightly.

'Who's calling me?' Sabine asks, still lost in her dream. She's speaking off-camera, she can't see herself, any more than she can see where the insistent call is coming from: 'Sa/bine Sa/bine Sa/bine...'

'Anyway,' she says, 'I don't like my name, I don't like anything my parents gave me.'

On the ground is an intact pelvis, it's a chalky white and there are words engraved on the surface of the hipbones, it looks like an immense petrified bird, its wings ocellated with letters. The words are written in a language Sabine doesn't know, but she can still decipher some scraps by running the tips of her fingers over the letters. 'Sabine, from Latin *sabina*, the savin, a bush of the juniper species... in the Mediterranean... poisonous if wrongly used... convulsions, stomach pains, haemorrhages... scaly needles and...' The bony butterfly comes to life, flaps its wings and takes off ponderously. 'It's a swallowtail,' says Georges, appearing in the dreamer's field of vision, 'a giant swallowtail, but it's lost its colours. And I lost my lottery ticket. Because of you. You always lose everything, idiot!' He shrugs his shoulders. Sabine wakes with a start, her shoulders quivering convulsively.

She doesn't really know where she is, she doesn't recognise her bedroom. Oh yes, she tells herself, I'm in the sitting-room. It's still dark, she doesn't know what time it is. She feels a bit feverish. I must have caught cold, outside. She snuggles down under the blanket, but she can't get the last words she heard in her dream out of her head. Marie, stretched out beside her, is breathing in long sighs and shifting about a lot, as if she were trying to find a position conducive to sleep. Eventually Sabine gets up and goes to have a smoke in an armchair, wrapped up in the travelling rug she had on the sofa.

Towards midday the boys arrive back in the courtyard of the house, sounding their horns and bawling out their current catchphrase: 'Happy gabuzomeu!' this time in place of good morning. As it's a fine day, they set up a table in the garden, in the shade of a lime tree, for lunch. They wait a while for Pierre Zébreuze, but when he still doesn't appear, they start the meal without him, finishing it in the same way. As she serves coffee, Sabine expresses her concern about his absence, no one having seen him since the previous day. 'He left in such a funny way', she says, 'so abruptly and... I don't know...' She tells them how she and Marie came across him the previous evening, as if rooted to the top of the stairs, still wearing his costume. The way he stood there, looking as if he were at the end of his tether, they assumed he was playing the fool and burst out laughing. All of a sudden he dashed down the stairs four at a time and shot out of the house, leaving his clothes in a bundle on the landing. They'd called him, but to no avail, he seemed to have disappeared into thin air. Where could he have gone in that outfit, and without the keys to his flat, which were in his jacket pocket? His moped was still parked by the gate. 'Well,' René said, 'he'll have hitched a lift or gone on foot, he loves walking.' Henri adds that Pierre doesn't need his keys to get in, he's always forgetting to close doors behind him and Sébastien suggests he might have gone to see a mistress who happens to live in that area. They all take up this idea and make jokes about the disappearing Gibi going on to finish the night in some pleasant den of vice. Finally Charlam, exasperated by the way the Poacher dominates the discussion, even if by being made fun of, bursts out with, 'Do you think we could change the subject? There are others that are decidedly more interesting!' But he's not unhappy with the suggestion that the beggar had a mistress in the area, it will mortify his hypocritical daughter-in-law, whom he is observing out of the corner of his eye with a long, hard look. He notices that she is very pale, with dark rings under her eyes and a preoccupied look. Noted down and may be used in evidence, he thinks with disdain.

During the afternoon everyone departs, leaving Sabine, Marie and Louma. Pierre doesn't reappear that evening, nor the next day or on any of the following days. Finally Sabine reports his disappearance to the police, but they tell her that, as an adult, Zébreuze is free to go where he likes and to do as he likes, and since he is not thought to be dangerous, the inquiry will be pursued slowly and with minimal resources. When she tells Henri, René and Hector about his disappearance, they're surprised but not particularly concerned. Going off without telling anyone is certainly odd, especially as Pierre seemed his usual self the last time they saw him and they'd all had great fun rehearsing their show. But Pierre can be unpredictable and, anyway, they know almost nothing at all about his private life. Perhaps he'd taken off on impulse or, like the Gibis and the Shadoks in the cartoon series, had decided he wanted a change of planet — they'd all felt the same urge during adolescence, each in his own way. That would be it, deep down inside Pierre was an eternal adolescent.

Charlam, for his part, is savouring what he regards as a victory. So that was all it took to get rid of the Poacher, a few drops of saliva and, poof! the undesirable had disappeared: erased, dissolved like a nasty grease-stain. He must have felt pretty guilty to decamp like that at the first warning sign. Charlam goes through the scene again in his mind, it only lasted a blink of the eye, a snap of the fingers, the click of a camera. Just the time it took to spit, that's all. In his mind's eye he sees the fellow's mouth with greasepaint plastered all over it as he wished him a casual good night, his narrow shoulders and the dumbfounded look in his colourless eyes when he responded to the two-faced bastard's meek-and-mild smile with an honest gob of spit. The final scene as described by that silly goose, Sabine — the Poacher caught in an invisible trap, struggling to free himself, then running off like some fowl that has just had its head cut off — is really something to gladden his heart. She and Marie took what was his crushing defeat for a game. But Charlam will remain on guard, if ever the fugitive should dare to return he'll make him beat a hasty retreat — and for good!

Allons z'enfants…

The tree screams inside the tree, the tree prays inside the tree, it has no other way of speaking than that: being a tree. What is a tree? What is it that leaks out, endlessly, in a frenzy of forests, of ships, of poems?
If I wasn't there…

Roger Giroux

1

He ran a lot that night, the big gander with half its feathers gone, wheezing for breath, his chest dripping with sweat and drizzle. He ran at random, zigzagging through the night until he was out of breath and his muscles gave way. Then he just let himself fall, his heart spent, his body broken. He dropped to his knees, then his torso slumped forward and he collapsed face down, his arms forming a circle round his head. He didn't cry, or shout, or groan, he didn't think or dream, he sank into a state of torpor, his mouth and eyes half open on top of the mud. On his lips, against his teeth there was that bitter, slimy taste of sodden soil and in his eyes that brownish black. His remaining scraps of consciousness have decomposed in the mud, the dullness.

He got up towards dawn and took off the ski-suit in which he was still half clothed, it was wet and uncomfortable as it stuck to his skin. His mind was still benumbed, covered in mud, no thoughts could form in it. He had returned to the soil, he was nothing but the outline of a man moulded in the clay and he thought with his clayey skin. He took off all his clothes so that he could breathe better with his whole body, sniff the air like an animal checking for the approach of a predator; the only ones he feared were human. But his sense of smell was not really sharpened yet and, above all, his pores had the same smell as that of the predators he so feared; trying to flee them, he was fleeing from himself.

He kept on walking for a long time, his feet were scraped raw. He saw some rails, he went down to the track and followed it to the edge of a marshalling yard. There were more rails there, they multiplied, describing sweeping curves. There were lines of tank wagons — dozens of grey paps in long rows — trucks and goods trains. In one place he heard an indistinct clatter, movement, and smelt a strong, warm odour. He opened the door of one of the wagons the noises and the stench were coming from, hauled himself up and closed the door behind him. It was crammed with bullocks pawing the floor, mooing in a muted chorus. He threaded his way through them and squatted down on the straw in a corner. It was nice and warm among the animals. Some time in the morning the train set off and continued for hours, stopping at several stations.

The stowaway was discovered when the bullocks were taken out of the truck — a naked man, covered in filth from head to foot, huddled up at the back of the wagon. He stank of urine-soaked dung, of human and bovine sweat. 'Who the hell's that?! Does he think he's little Jesus in his crib?' one of those who found him exclaimed. A Jesus who had somewhat run to seed, hirsute and dirty, stupefied into the bargain, more of a Jesus who had descended into hell and couldn't find the exit. Unless it was the ass from the crib, come to provide a skinny counterweight to the herd of bullocks? He didn't reply to any of their questions — was he a foreigner? — did not utter a single word — was he dumb? — showed no sign of intelligence — was he an imbecile? If he was, he appeared to be an inoffensive one. Given the state he was in, they took him to the hospital and, once he'd been through A & E, they transferred him to the psychiatric ward. All their attempts to find out who this person was, to pierce his anonymity, led nowhere. At the beginning he was given various nicknames: the Unknown Man from the Crib, the Cattleman, the Maggot, the Nudist, The Bullock-Ass, finally Jesus the Bullock. That was the nickname he ended up with. Jesus the Bullock, it fitted him, at least half fitted him, for if he had the innocence of the former and the placidity of the latter, he possessed neither the grace of the one nor the strength of the other.

To tell the truth, he possessed nothing at all, his nakedness was even more extensive internally than physically, at a stroke he had reached the bottom, the void. And he sat down in the void, the way old people sit on a park bench, simply to pass the time, waiting for the hours to pass, drop by drop, and life, silently, gently. But each of those drops of time that goes by in slow motion is saturated with memories, with a mixture of light and shade, with murmurings, like the drops oozing through the roofs of caves which, when they are full, ripe like grapes bursting with juice, detach themselves and fall. It's a long fall, strangely heavy and light, unobtrusive and shining, silent and resounding through the rocky chasm. That is how stalactites and stalagmites are formed. When they meet, a spiral column rises, a huge umbilical cord linking the depths with the summit, the darkness with the threshold of daylight. The process can last thousands of years. In Jesus the Bullock it lasted eight years which, on the human scale, is almost equivalent.

2

In the days following the disappearance of Pierre Zébreuze, the tennis shoes and ski-suit he was wearing when he ran off were found in a small wood close to the house. Shoes, socks and clothing were lying on the ground among the dead leaves, spattered with mud, already spotted with mould, but no bloodstains were found. Had he decided to return to a state of nature, become an impromptu wild man of the woods? He wouldn't have been able to hide there for long, the spinney was neither dense nor extensive. Unless he'd dug himself a burrow, which wasn't very likely. It was equally unlikely that he'd left the wood completely without clothes, someone walking in the nude through the fields or along a road would soon have been noticed. The deduction was that he must have thrown his clothes away after having changed, there or elsewhere, and had taken off for some reason that was suspected of being rather shady, especially after the insinuations in the statement Charles-Amédée Bérynx had insisted on making, and headed for some unknown destination.

Sabine and Marie were the only ones not to be satisfied with this non-conclusion. They had witnessed the scene where he had looked at the end of his tether, followed by his distraught flight and had immediately cast off their initial great misunderstanding. They had gone over the scene in their minds again and again, scrutinising it in minute detail. By examining and dissecting Pierre's looks and behaviour, they had eventually come across tiny signs which ought to have warned them, if they hadn't let themselves be carried away by an outburst of uncontrollable laughter. The half-skinned Gibi had had a wild, distressed look, his body was racked with shivers. Something they were unaware of had happened, he must have been given some terrible news that had hit him hard, but by whom? By himself, perhaps, a sudden revelation that had come to him, emerging from the depths of oblivion? Sabine herself had occasionally had moments when feelings that had disappeared suddenly burst into consciousness, revived, sunken memories leapt up without warning to seize her by the heart. But even if they took her breath away, set her mind in a whirl, suspended thought, she had never succumbed to the attack, she had regained her balance somehow or other and continued on her normal way, concealing her inner turmoil. Marie, after all her wild fits, had experimented with a brief, intense seismic upheaval and when she came out of it, she had cut herself off from the vehement, tormented side of herself. But then she had felt relieved, freed of a burden. However, all the possibilities they worked out as they kept on going over the evening again and again lead nowhere.

They went to Pierre's apartment. They had some scruples about entering it when he wasn't there, but they hoped that it would help them, that they'd find some information, some clues, even a message he'd left. The flat had two rooms, very little furniture, no knickknacks, the order and austerity were positively monastic. In a cupboard they discovered a neat pile of parcels, still in their gift-wrapping; he appeared never to have opened them. In the kitchen there was little crockery and little food, a few tins in a row on a shelf, a jar of currants, a crate of potatoes covered with a newspaper, a plate with fruit that was already rotting and some bottles of wine in a rack. Opened packets of cigarettes were lying around in several places, Sabine took one and lit it. I was a Gitane, without filter, she usually smoked Virginia and she immediately stubbed out the bitter-tasting cigarette. They looked at the books on the three shelves made of deal planks set on bricks. Lots of history, a few novels borrowed from the town library, guide books to the regions of France, a collection of legends from the Pyrenees, some dictionaries, including one on architecture, two poetry anthologies, some books and magazines about painting. Mainly contemporary painting, Klee, Chagall, Braque, Dufy, Mondrian, Matisse, Vlaminck, Picasso, Soutine, de Staël, Tàpies, Pollock. A reproduction of a picture by Klee was pinned to the wall over the sink, almost at eye-level when you were standing in front of it: an abstract landscape in pastel, all horizontal and vertical lines, some diverging slightly, broken, evoking a bird's-eye view of fields and stretches of water.

In the bedroom there was a reproduction, in a very large format, of a painting stuck to the wall facing the bed. The painter's name was not given, but he took sparseness even farther than Klee; the picture — a blaze of yellow and orange with a white line running across highlighted with grey-green, the whole heightened with splashes of green — called to mind a patch of sunlight. So that was what Pierre liked to see when he woke up or as he was going to bed: a tall rectangle of sunlight; and when he washed the dishes: a checkerboard landscape gently vibrating to the rhythm of ochre, pale green, mauves, lavender and flax blue, straw and quince yellow. Space, colour, light, nothing figurative.

In the drawer of the bedside table Marie found a slim cardboard folder with a woman's name written on it in capitals with a black felt-tip: Zélie. She immediately remembered the stories Pierre used to think up for her and the Zélie he had created as a companion for her friend Zoé. Marie felt their former collusion justified her in taking the file, which must contain tales dating from the days of her childhood, perhaps even some she hadn't seen. She rolled it up carefully and stuffed it in her bag without telling her mother what she'd found. She was determined to be the first to read the stories which, anyway, were intended for her, or at least had been. At the same time Sabine, too, was committing a minor theft, unknown to her daughter: a little cardboard-backed album with photographs. Leafing through it, she had seen that it contained the one of her four children grouped round Pierre dressed up as Father Christmas. So each of them went home with a little prize hidden in her bag which they were determined to appraise alone.

As she had all those years ago when faced with the Polaroid Andrée had brought back from the Galeries Clasquin, Sabine got a magnifying glass to examine the photos more closely. There were more of places than of people — three of the same house taken from different angles and several of a garden, including some close-ups of trees. In one of the trees, a lime with an imposing spread, she saw that a tree-house had been built in the branches. There were also some that had been taken in the zoo showing avenues, aviaries, a couple of buffaloes with black coats, a bison, immense tortoises. These latter had been photographed from close up, the head of one of the tortoises had been very carefully centred, its disturbingly expressionless half-closed eyes could be clearly seen. The picture made Sabine think both of an old man's head, shrunk and dried, and of that of a deformed foetus with cracked, horny skin — a suggestion of life fossilised in a tegument that was half woody, half mineral, a condensation of consciousness on the surface of dense, callous matter.

A few portraits finally bring a little humanity back to the album: some of a brunette with close-set, black eyes, a piercing look and a curious charm, and some of a tall, thin man Sabine at first took for Pierre, but on a closer look realised was someone else, his father or a close relative. One photo was of a merry little blonde girl, standing on the wooden seat of a swing hanging from the branch of a tree, another of a girl wearing a floral dress with a broad, tight belt emphasising her slim waist. This girl, or young woman, was standing with one knee slightly bent and her arms at head height holding the edge of an open-weave straw hat. Her face, mottled with splashes of sunlight, was difficult to make out but one could tell that she was smiling. Another portrait, perhaps of the same person, was equally difficult to make out because the subject had her hands raised, fingers spread in a fan, in front of her face: one wide-open eye was staring at the lens through the V formed by two fingers. The look from this eye, set apart from the face as a whole, sparkled with a mixture of impertinence, artlessness and bluntness. Sabine put these three last photos, the little girl and the two young women, side by side and examined them for a long time, looking to see if she could find any link between them, but the only connection she managed to establish seemed to be the reduced visibility, either blurred by a lacework of leaves or straw, or broken up by a lattice of fingers. Then came the photo of the Father Christmas with the children. Sabine was profoundly moved by the fact that Pierre had had a copy made and stuck it in this very personal album, at the same time hurt that she herself didn't appear in the collection of portraits. Did she mean nothing to Pierre, did he not judge her worthy of inclusion in the little coterie of his loved ones? The hurt was puerile, as she was well aware, but nonetheless real.

It was possible the tall thin man and the brunette were his parents but who was the girl? A fiancée he'd had in his youth, a lost love, a girl friend? She wasn't even sure whether there was just the one or two of them, all that she knew was that he had told her, and repeated it several times, that he was completely alone in the world, that he had had neither brothers nor sisters, nor cousins, nor children. Could he have had just this one love, an old love now? Though what was there to say that it was an old love? But she didn't dare share these questions with Marie, she felt ashamed, guilty, without being able to say of what or why. Of being in love with Pierre, when she had always refused to let herself be, to feel jealous for no reason, to suspect her own daughter of being in love with Pierre as well? Unsure of herself, she said nothing.

The dossier Marie took did contain something she hadn't seen, but it was put together in a very disorganised fashion, being composed of disparate sheets of paper, pages torn out of exercise books of varying size and quality, bits of paper picked up anywhere, scraps of cardboard and even some pieces of lavatory paper, all covered in writing and drawing, sometimes just unconnected words, pencil sketches and, separated by a divider, a few pen-and-wash drawings. It wasn't Pierre's writing and, moreover, several of the drawings were signed 'Zélie'. Most of the pen-and-wash drawings were of a female face, always the same, of which it was difficult to tell the age, the extreme youth of the subject being in each case infested with, even engulfed by distortions, exaggerations, wounds, signs of great age. The only constant was the very rounded eyelids and the circumflex arc of the eyebrows and, even more, the look in the eyes which seemed an extreme compression of opposites — transparent and clouded, fixed and flickering, artless and violent, defiant and imploring.

If the fragments Marie managed to decipher did not tell her much about the identity of the girl with the discordant look or about her connection with Pierre, she sensed a relationship between her and the person she herself had been until very recently which was so intimate she at times thought she had written certain sentences herself, almost as if words, cries, questions had been stolen at a distance in space and time. She found certain details disturbing: Zélie sometimes distanced herself from her own self, turning 'I' into a third-person pronoun, and she left punctuation out. The lack of full stops at the end of sentences gave Marie the feeling she was in danger of falling off at the end of each one, of plunging down into the yawning gulf beneath the surface of words.

3

Something inside my mouth is moving like a gentle breeze

I has left without even taking the time to be born

*Careful when biting into an apple a plum a peach! They could easily
bite back
A storm is silently rumbling in fruit stones*

*The pangs of beauty: to seize the moment when an eyelash falls onto
the wood of a table*

*to hear in the distance the sweet
and monotonous creaking of a pulley*

*to see as you walk along a street
a tuft of saxifrage or golden cress on the bars of a basement window*

*What is telling you that I am not much older than most of you beginning
with you my ancestors
saddled with age-old wisdom which to your novices' eyes makes me
seem insane?*

*The day sharpens its terror the day whets its knives on the contempt of
right-thinking people for bastard and impertinent girls*

*They have robbed me of my words of the right and the strength to hurl
them wherever and whenever I see fit
words to stone their stupidity their lies their flatulences*

By way of baptism I have been anointed with spit

*This evening a fly came and died on the floor of my bedroom
long death throes*

*I has watched them with total empathy devoid of all emotion: the fly the
death throes me watched assiduously*

*My genitals — pink and blond outside nocturnal inside, and so soft so
tender delicious to touch my genitals with the pretty closed lips know
so many songs chirp with so many fevers like my mouth would I have
these violent bleeds if they hadn't sewn up my lips all my lips
Oh my martyred mouths!
Who are they making fun of at the back of my throat? Who is it they
are denigrating maligning with their gurgling sputtering? It's me of
course it's me!*

*The night when they put my mother in the ground — a very pure night
For it is by night that You and You buried her Put her straight in the
earth without a coffin clothed in a sheet Her wedding sheet? If so —
which wedding?*

Days in aphelion They keep me at an infinite distance from life

*How can one open a book? The danger of freeing wild beasts is too
great
How can one open one's mouth? A great poem at war lies decimated
on my tongue
How can one open one's eyes? I am too afraid that all I will see will be
the shadow of myself And my shadow is a nail stuck in the sun*

*Someone inside me is talking to unknown people talking softly talking
in a dark-red language talking endlessly sometimes sniggering*

*The horrifying splendour of a lavender-blue sky seen behind a lattice
of words deprived of a page to disport themselves run about on*

My mother taught me something terrible: you can die of laughter

The wind always tastes of rust it only comes into my room after having

Sylvie Germain

licked the bars on the window
With these bars the sky is permanently wearing striped pyjamas I have
come to doubt whether there is a body in those pyjamas of iron of
emptiness
A celestial body
I would so love to caress the skin of the sky the pinkness of its dawns
scratch its azure torso lick the blood of its evenings wrap myself in the
purple of the nights ride the clouds bite the wind chew the flashes of
lightning It will come

I am a state of war that rhymes with Amor It's a very poor very crude
very forbidden rhyme

I listen to absence sprouting like a bamboo shoot drunk with growing
True true the big bamboo!

He fathered me   You brought me up
             She — between He and You
She so alone among us all She and me She contorted with laughter
contortoised with laughter And You? You delivered me
Delivered me up to oblivion as one is delivered up to the enemy

I was forced to swap the convulsions of laughter for those of electric
shock treatment and I lost everything in the exchange

To go barenecked in the chilly wind to cut the carotid artery to peel the
jugular vein

In the belly of the earth: immense night In the belly of a woman:
profound night In the belly of love: night in spate In the belly of my
head: night night and night In the belly of a tortoise: reptilian night
half carnal half telluric In the belly of God? — us, the living and the
dead
In the belly of the name of God: absolute night
In the belly of language: branching darkness All these darknesses form

107

just the one they join up in a circle dance the farandole

Catastrophe of sweetness: the Christian names of my two fathers and that of my mother
But what use are names without bodies?

Spirals and curls — a little fire is quietly smoking on the tip of my tongue

My two mouths have a lot to say — the visible one and the hidden one
Forcing them to remain silent corrodes them with icy saliva with acid tears overwhelms them with stellar concretions

I is seeking the path that will allow me to get to the point of it at last
To the high point?

I has to be sensible be quiet knuckle under I receives so many orders pieces of advice threats I couldn't give a shit about them I goes all out putting her life on the line to not give a shit about them
Put my life on the line

God — a name slobbered soiled belched stammered snivelled thundered pissed vomited as the case may be by too many stupid bastards to be used any more Necessary to find a new and underlineable name Given the impossibility of achieving that it is a matter of urgency that we shut up Breathing is sufficient to call upon the name of the Nameless.
Breathing breathing — the purest of prayers

Today I broke a tooth trying to bite the bars on the window I'm taking great care to keep the taste of iron on my scraped tongue

Two fathers — one gave me his eyes the other his look or vice versa who knows

I learn to cry out in silence to hate in neutral amply the way we breathe

Sylvie Germain

to love Nothing

Asylum and zoo Animals and lunatics our looks are the same they shine with rot

Zélie Zélie Zélie however much I shout murmur write my name no one answers even me I has run off

Every evening I have to gather up with my bare hands splinters of reality that has been broken by someone during the day the night I stick them together with gold resin but the gold becomes tarnished in the light and the resin weeps and I have to start all over again

You — neither you nor words will have saved me

In my belly a globe of night is turning All women since the origins have carried a globe of night under the skin of their belly
Globe of reddening night globe of aqueous night globe of ravenous scrawny night
Lunar globe terrestrial globe solar globe uterine globe globe of the breast globe of fire oral globe globe of wind — Globus!
What do men know of the night? They only enter it as intruders

Do you know?
No you know nothing not even what you are doing especially not what you are doing and still you do it conscientiously and perseveringly

I'm paying the price of the sperm in perpetuity

I hear the sound of footsteps in my brain little bird's footsteps
and creaking lapping sighing stridor
stridor stridence, stridulation strangulation

By dint of dying and of being here all the time I have no idea where I am at Even whether I am full stop

Waiting in neutral waiting for nothing
Grandiose terror

My mother is at rest with the tortoises She lies under their heavy belly
heavy with more than a century heavy with patience and boredom
heavy with obstinate expectation with no conclusion no consolation
The biggest tortoise, their monster queen, is called Fantine

Tomorrow is not another day tomorrow is the punishment which
ceaselessly increases by today

I call you Judas it's a statement of fact Judas was not the bastard people
say he was Judas was neither treacherous nor venal nor an informer
Judas was a simpleton a moron
it is with the best of intentions that he committed the worst of crimes
thinking he was helping his friend speed up his emergence from the
shadows hasten his triumph his glory Crash bang everything came a
cropper his friend did emerge from the shadows but he tumbled through
a trapdoor straight down into darkness Hey there! On your feet you
dead guys! and off they all went hobbling along somewhere else
Elsewhere that's where the safeguard is
I don't want to see you any more you kindly assassin
Never again neither here nor Elsewhere
Oh! especially not Elsewhere
Elsewhere — expanding Globus

Fantine Elephantine Phantom Infantile — Cooee! Mummy lying
clandestinely in chelonian earth

Exquisite oral pleasure: to utter in muted tones — passiflora fealty
mosaic shaft
rustling anaglyph meander lapis lazuli agave hierophant bandoneon

Double father and double error: the luminous one consigned to the
shadow the dark one exposed to the light of day The mistake has fallen

on me

Writing doesn't save anything, it only helps to delay the fatal moment

At lunchtime I plaited some blond tomato-coloured scoubidous out of spaghetti and my hair

4

That was where the collection of jottings, strewn by Zélie on any piece of paper that came to hand, stopped. As with the drawings, there was a theme running through these scattered lines, obsessions were hammered out, but there were too many gaps in the jigsaw for it to be put together so that it showed an identifiable face. Marie had no idea over what length of time these scraps spread, none of the sheets was dated and Zélie remained elusive. Had she even existed and if so, how old was she, was she still alive? The thing was that Marie, too, had scribbled moody notes when she was a child, caustic and scornful aphorisms under the name of Zoé. Who was hiding behind Zélie? It couldn't be Pierre. But then why had he chosen that name, evidently laden with pain and madness, to introduce into Marie's imaginary universe? There was poison in that figure, whether she was real or fictitious. Was Pierre, her thoughtful, devoted companion, whose patience was inexhaustible to the point of exasperation, a lot craftier than he appeared, had he taken pleasure in secreting venom extracted from this disturbed phantom called Zélie in Marie's imagination, or was he as much of a simpleton as the Judas denounced and absolved by the said Zélie? Absolved, but from a distance, without reconciliation.

Weary of this history burdened with enigmas, disappearances, incoherences, where the real and the illusory, the insane and the possible were constantly intertwined — knit one purl one — Marie suddenly decided to cease her investigations. Good riddance to Pierre, wherever he had decided to go without thinking it was worth telling anyone, good riddance to the poor Judas who had run off into the night. So, following the example of the police, she had closed the case and put away the folder, with its meagre elements, that she had purloined. And it was her own past, her old terrors and her fits of rage that she buried with it. It completed the break with Pierre, and even more with the angry part of herself, which had started a few months earlier on the day when she had rejected his present. She was determined not to give any more encouragement to those voices that had haunted her for so long, she had to silence everything that threatened to make her relapse and that included the cries and laments of the siren Zélie. She finally applied herself at school so as to concentrate her attention on other things.

The following year, having obtained her *baccalauréat,* Marie left Hourfeuville and went to Paris to start a course at the School of Applied Arts. Louma retired as well, no longer being needed to look after the children.

Alone in the big house, Sabine immediately devoted even more of her time and energy to her work than in the past. Her shop prospered, the meaning of her life narrowed correspondingly. One evening, returning to the deserted house, late as was her habit, she had a physical sense of the emptiness of her home and her existence. It had grabbed her by the back of the neck, as if a hand had come down on her with a cold, firm grip to put her under arrest. She gave a stifled cry and turned round sharply. There was no one, just her own reflection in the big wall mirror at the other end of the sitting-room. Taking slow steps, she walked towards the mirror, her reflection getting progressively larger and clearer, like someone going along a straight, narrow street towards another person. But unlike the two passers-by, who avoid looking each other in the eye, merely give each other a furtive sidelong glance, she went right up to the mirror, planted herself in front of it and gave herself a long, hard look. Since childhood she had looked at herself thousands and thousands of times, often very closely, sometimes scrutinising this or that detail of her face or body, sometimes appraising the whole, her expression, her posture, the elegance of her outfit. But she had never looked at herself like this before. Like this: impromptu, without concern for her appearance, her complexion or her figure, her beauty, her bearing. Without concern for anyone or anything, especially not for the image she presented.

Like this: caught unawares, stripped bare by surprise, unsettled by amazement. And for the first time she saw her gaze, naked, free of herself. An intense, calm gaze, unreacting, looking straight at her. Not at her, Sabine Bérynx, a mature woman, but at the living being that she was, very simply, very powerfully. She, a living being, a person, a human. An ephemeron in the world, a transient in time, a mortal. A tiny mystery to be among billions of others, unique and insignificant, fleeting and immortal. A tremendous promise — but of what? She held her ground in face of this silent other she, withstood for a moment her look, radiant in its nakedness, implacable in its placidity, its patience, she heard the silent questions she was posing, listened to her appeal, welling up from the remotest fastnesses of time, from the very depths of her humanity, from the pores of her skin, the darkness of her pupils, the silvering of the mirror, from the moment, then she lowered her eyelids which were suddenly heavy, damp with embarrassment. How could one reply to such a look? Her own was gaping helplessly at the ground. Then she noticed her feet, down there, standing sensibly on the wooden floor: two feet, tired from having walked, marked time, carried her body all day long, two weary feet in their pretty, old-rose leather court shoes, and she smiled.

She took them off and studied her feet, lifting each one up in turn and twisting it this way and that; slim feet, nicely rounded, but the left one was already in the process of becoming ugly with the development of a reddish bunion and corns on her toes. She smiled — what a ridiculous state she was in! The answer to the question posed by her detached look came quickly, prompted by her feet: 'Up you get and off you go.' She had nothing else to say, nothing else to suggest. It seemed to her that the look relaxed a little, that its gravity became tinged with irony.

5

Sabine appointed a manager to run the shop and let her house; following the example of her children, she left. Her decision surprised and worried the family, especially Charlam who, immediately suspecting his daughter-in-law of pursuing some risky project, feared that with her abandoning the business and the family house in this way everything, that is the inheritance that was supposed to come to Georges' children one day, would go down the drain. He resorted to his favourite weapon, which was to arouse suspicion in his grandchildren, but although he had some response from René and Hector, he failed with Henri and, inevitably, with Marie.

The eldest of Georges' sons, on whom he had very early on set his patriarchal hopes, had freed himself from his influence several years ago now. Serious and docile as a boy, hardworking at school, he hardly questioned the authority, opinions and wishes of his grandfather, who knew how to flatter him and quietly gain his allegiance. Thus he came to share Charlam's antipathy towards Pierre Zébreuze, the employee who, recruited by his mother, had too quickly become a friend, a close friend, and had established a special relationship with Marie, his insufferable little sister. A man who was too obliging not to be self-seeking, too involved with the family not to have inveigled his way in like the worm in the bud. Henri had made Charlam's opinion his own. One day, goaded by Charlam's insinuations about the supposed affair between his mother and the 'Poacher', he had secretly got into his flat with the intention of discovering evidence of his hypocrisy, his dishonesty. All he had found there was a modest, orderly apartment, some books on art and history, great simplicity. He had been intrigued by the piles of gift-wrapped packages in a cupboard and had managed to open some without tearing or crumpling the wrapping paper, hoping to find compromising items such as stolen jewels, bundles of purloined banknotes, weapons or packets of drugs. He had found nothing of the sort, merely the things which had been wrapped up in them in the shops selling clothes, souvenirs, toiletries, office accessories, DIY equipment. Practical presents, cheap, innocuous. Henri had carefully done the packages up again, less disappointed at not having found anything illicit than disconcerted at Zébreuze's oddness in not opening the presents he had been given. Was he completely indifferent to things or was he mean enough to recycle the goods by giving them as presents to others?

Before leaving the flat, where, despite his detective zeal as one who was very biassed against the tenant, he had found no evidence of fraud, he had taken one last look round. It was then that he was struck by the patch of yellow on the wall of the bedroom which he hadn't noticed before, even though he been in the room several times to rummage through things. Yet it was a huge patch — a rectangular pool of light cut out of the body of the sun. It was facing the bed, more imposing and luminous than a window. Henri went up to the giant poster until he could place his hands on it. He felt a strange sensation, as if the yellow and the orange of the picture were caressing his palms, gently radiating under his skin, stimulating his heart, flowing into his eyes. It had made him forget the reason for his visit, his suspicions, his prejudice against the man who had ensnared his mother, had seduced his bitch of a sister. He had forgotten everything and had delicately caressed the picture as if it were a back, an arm, a woman's stomach, hair, a child's cheek, a young man's chest, a sunbeam, the skin of a dream. And he had felt happy, grave and light at the same time, gently dazzled. Then he had stretched out on the bed facing the solar picture, the name of which he didn't know, and contemplated it for a long time.

Staring at it, he had the impression a face was showing on the surface, but he couldn't say whose. Not a specific face, just the possibility of an advent, of the very bare, shimmering glory of a face too intense to be depicted.

An idea had suddenly burst into his mind which, although preposterous, compelled acceptance as a statement of the obvious: a man who has chosen such a painting to bear him company in the solitude of his bedroom cannot be truly bad. Calmed by this absurd conviction, Henri had finally got up and left the flat. From that day on he had looked on Pierre Zébreuze with a different eye, relieved of prejudice, and had gradually established friendly relations with him, to the great displeasure of Charlam, who lost an ally. But Henri had never dared admit to Pierre that he had gone to his flat to search through his things, so that he had not been able to ask the name of the painter.

He had certainly been surprised by Pierre's flight into the darkness, but not alarmed; at the time he had no more accepted his mother's and Marie's fears than the spiteful insinuations made by Charlam. But as the days passed the disappearance started to worry him as well, he could find no explanation for Pierre's sudden flight, his abandoned clothes, the way he seemed to have vanished into thin air. Everything suggested that Pierre must have been murdered, without it being possible to understand either the reasons or the circumstances, nor how the body had been disposed of. But the investigation had been botched and produced no results, the file of the 'Zébreuze case' was in the pending tray, in suspended animation. For Henri, this 'case' was above all a nagging question: how can a man go, at a stroke and totally, from a presence to nothing, to silence? Had we no more substance than a puff of steam, no more importance than a speck of dust?

He took possession of the large poster from Pierre's bedroom when they had to clear out his flat, which the estate agents, tired of waiting for their tenant's return, had repossessed. There was a black sticker on the back of the reproduction, telling him at last who the painter was: Mark Rothko. A large-scale oil painting on canvas, painted in 1953. Henri could not but notice that it was the year of his birth. An insignificant detail basically but it strengthened the bond tying him to the picture. 'An image of the instant of my conception, of my gestation or of the dazzling light as I emerged from limbo?' he asked himself when he discovered the coincidence. But the real question was, how could he manage to feel, mind and body, in every fibre of his muscles, in his heart, in every nerve and down to his bones, in every fibril of his senses and every convolution of his brain the taste, the sound, the tone of this yellow, how could he enter into this incandescent splendour without dissolving in it, savour this light without losing his sight, his consciousness, his breath? How could he savour this light with absolute *understanding?* If he had had any aptitude for painting and drawing he would have ventured along that route, but he lacked the talent, he would remain a mere observer, a witness. He likes to look, to observe, he knows how to see. That, too, is a gift, less creative perhaps, more modest, but one which demands just as much work, concentration, patience. He ended up by training for a profession which suited his curiosity and his clear-sightedness as a witness: photojournalism.

It is Marie who is practising the art of drawing, but in a way she hadn't foreseen. One day she felt like reopening the cherry-red file where she had put all the tales Pierre had invented for her, and read them again dispassionately. Despite the clumsiness and naivety of some of his stories she felt they had a certain charm. She also reopened the cardboard folder she had taken from Pierre's room and examined the contents again — the drawings with their crazy scrawls, the scraps of language jotted down on bits of paper. Enough time had passed since she'd first seen these pages, the unease she'd suffered then had faded, she no longer felt threatened by the siren-song of the unknown girl called Zélie and was less preoccupied with the thought of Pierre. Learning to live alone, away from the family cocoon, and to submit to the discipline of study had allowed her to turn away from the burning-mirror where for a long time she had stirred the fire of her fears, her sorrows, her angers, eventually of her distress. A magic mirror that had finally become tarnished and no longer had the power to lure her.

The stories Pierre had thought up, which she had just reread without being moved or irritated by them, gave her the idea of rewriting and illustrating them, mixing in a few fragments stolen from Zélie, but cleansed of their reek of suffering. One summer she devoted her holiday to carrying out this project. The result was a short book embellished with simple, brightly coloured — predominantly red — drawings, entitled: *The Silly Things Zélie Did.* The first words were, 'At lunchtime I plaited some blond and tomato-coloured scoubidous out of spaghetti and my hair…' The setting was innocuous, the scene took place in a school dining hall and it continued with a series of zany tricks played by a saucy little girl called Zélie.

This summer's pastime turned out to be more serious than she had imagined. On the advice of a friend she sent her manuscript to publisher of children's books and five months later she received a contract. *The Silly Things Zélie Did* was published in a small square format and sold very well. The publisher encouraged Marie to think up new comic adventures and misadventures for her little devil. At the moment she's working on her third book, each beginning with a sentence from the 'Zélie file' diverted from its source or, to be more precise, from its well, to go romping through the imagination, and all published under the name of Zoé Zébrynx.

They continue to be successful. Since her first book came out she has worn the little chain Pierre gave her for her seventeenth birthday round her ankle.

6

Sabine settled in a village by the sea on the Cotentin peninsula, on the top floor of a tall building. Beyond the windows of her apartment: sky and water, a swirl of cloud and light, space as far as the eye can see. Sabine lives in an aquarium of silence suspended in a void that is in constant movement. In summer she gets up at daybreak, opening her eyes on the expanse of sky still veiled in night, but with a very thin veil, quivering with pink, with glimmers of straw-coloured light. She watches the glimmers gently rise to a flood in waves of gold that swell, intensify and break in ever wider, ever brighter surges. All day until evening the light displays wonderful undulations of vivid blue silk shot through with pink, saffron, lilac, crimson, ruby. In the winter she gets up before daybreak and watches the semidark dissolve under the very slow rise of the light appearing in muted sheets. The sky becomes satiny with shimmers of pearl, old ivory and silver turning to ash grey before finally being suffused with purple. Every season has it own tint, every hour its particular texture in this endless dialogue between the sea and the clouds, this exchange woven by sun, wind and rain. And even when the song of the light subsides, when it darkens until at times if comes close to foundering in a flat calm of grey, a hint of brightness always subsists, as if, by some mysterious inversion, a luminous glaze had been applied as a foundation over the immensity of the sky so that every colour that later appears, even a leaden grey or black, still remains luminescent.

Her children come to visit her from time to time, always separately, each anxious to see her alone to make the most of her presence, which has something fluid, unsettling about it, something between melancholy, serenity and kindness. Initially they were surprised and, above all, worried to see her choose a life in the slow lane, she who used to be so busy, always in a hurry. In isolating herself in this way was she not risking to become like Aunt Shh!. But when they ask her if she doesn't get bored, she says no, she never gets bored — there are the skies.

There are the skies, the sea, the birds and the wind and that's enough for her. This geographical migration has allowed her to keep her former life, which was threatening to grow stale, fossilised, at a distance; the life she led before Georges' death, and then the long path through mourning, the boundless energy spent in work and in her worries about her sons and, above all, her daughter, her feeling of abandonment, of uselessness after they left and Pierre disappeared.

Her life, all of a jumble, poorly tied up since her birth, too soon encumbered with responsibilities and worries, profoundly shaken by the loss of her husband, then that, equally sudden, of her friend, perhaps the only one she'd ever had — well, now she was untying it, letting it rest, pursue its course without constraint, with room to breathe. It would last as long as she found it meaningful and pleasant. A few months perhaps, or even her whole life. From now on that was going to be her way of being alive: standing upright, just as she had declared spontaneously in front of the mirror where her reflection had put a mute question to her. He response wasn't as silly as she had thought at the time, she had taken herself at her own word and acted on it. She had withdrawn from time, from other people, from herself, the better to observe them, to measure their flow, their substance, their consistency, the better to take soundings of the unknown part. She was savouring simply being alive.

When the lease of the house and the contract for the management of the shop expired, she didn't renew them but passed the properties on to two of her sons who were keen to run them after having completed their studies and several placements, one in business, the other in catering. She decided to use the sum Georges won on the lottery, that she had stubbornly kept hidden, consigned to oblivion. But the oubliette was a bank account and her little nest-egg had swelled considerably while sleeping there for so long. Since she finally felt able to take possession of this money, which was sufficient to allow her to live as she pleased, she could well afford to dispose of her properties for the benefit of her children. Finally, if she accepted the money from the piece of 'luck' which had immediately turned into a disaster, it was less as wealth than as a chance of detaching, effacing herself.

René took over the business his parents created some twenty years before and Hector rearranged the family home to open a restaurant there which he runs together with his young wife and the help of Louma. Henri, having chosen a nomadic profession, only comes to Hourfeuville occasionally for mostly fairly short stays; he has converted the old garden shed into a little chalet, while Marie, who spends most of her time in Paris, has set up a studio for herself in the loft. Each of them has a place of their own in their childhood home and even Louma has resumed her role of guardian angel of the household. Only Sabine keeps her distance, now more than ever she is a woman on the margin, on a tightrope, a mother wandering on the fringe of her family, a solitary.

*

She goes to Hourfeuville for Christmas and birthday celebrations, family gatherings, but she doesn't stay for long, she doesn't feel at home there any more. Louma, having been allowed to replace her, has come to take her function as a stand-in mother very seriously and behaves more and more as mistress of the house, treating Sabine as a guest, an honoured guest, of course, but transient. And then Charlam has made himself at home in Hourfeuville, making frequent — and long — stays there. He has managed to assert his influence, which he failed to do with Henri, over the twins, he is unsparing with his advice and has put his stamp on even the most intimate aspects of their lives; thus Hector has called his daughter Charlotte and René his son Charles-Georges, which has already become Charlorges. The tradition is being carried on, the patrimony is safe, order has finally been restored, the future is secure, Charlam is satisfied. Though only partly, for he is unhappy with other members of the family, first and foremost Marie, of course, who since she was a child has let no opportunity pass of drawing attention to herself with her outrageous behaviour. At present it's by inventing little stories no sensible person can make head or tail of, illustrated with nasty little drawings, no more than scrawls, which she has the gall to intend for children. The worst thing is that the kids and their parents love them, just as those horrible Shadoks appealed to people of all ages all those years ago. At least she does it under a pseudonym, but even the one she's chosen is grotesque: Zoé Zébrynx, how idiotic! A hybrid of zebra and lynx, a mishmash of squiffy and barmy, or what? And then that little chain she wears on her ankle, how vulgar!

As for Sabine, he resents the fact that she's left and that she's so determined to keep herself to herself. True, she's never shown any interest in or respect for the family, the clan, the heritage. Anyway, what's she living on now that she isn't working any longer? Is she being kept by some lover? Basically Charlam has never liked his daughter-in-law, with her icy beauty, fiercely independent yet capable of crawling to any Tom, Dick or Harry, like that tramp of a gigolo she employed, he's forgotten his name, but not the term he used for him, the 'Poacher'. No, he certainly doesn't like Sabine, despite the fact that, without ever having been able to admit it to himself, he's always admired her. He doesn't like her because he's never managed to make her submit to him. But behind this hurt pride there is a sharper wound: his failure to inspire filial affection in her.

Édith, too, has become a source of irritation to him. What can have got into the woman? She's left her stiffness behind, her perpetual migraines, her phobia about noise, she's cut her hair very short and dyed it a copper colour since it's gone white, in dress she's started to show the imagination everyone assumed she lacked and, after Grelot was killed in an accident, she got a new dog, Liquorice, a big strong beast with a black coat and a tremendous bass voice it uses all the time. And this woman, who spent all her time reading or lying down with every kind of headache, cloistered in silence, has started going out, travelling, bustling about here, there and everywhere. She's doing courses in archery and has taken up hang-gliding. Why not boxing and putting the shot while she's at it? The silly goose has waited until she's sixty, an age when people normally quieten down, to spend or, rather, waste, all the energy she'd saved. To Charlam this outburst of belated youth in his sister is as ridiculous and out of place as Sabine's turning in on herself — in her case prematurely — is saddening. This ludicrous exchange of behaviour between the two women becomes neither of them.

And then there's Henri, who has chosen a profession Charlam considers too risky, 'roughhouse photographer' as he contemptuously calls it. What business of his are all these bloody quarrels in Africa, in Asia, in Latin America, in the Near East? And anyway, what is there 'near' about that distant East, so chaotic and ferociously fratricidal? Europe has had its share, and more, of conflict and killing. At least he, Charlam, has had his fill of carnage. The First World War cast its great shadow over his adolescence, the Second, twenty years later brought back the shadow, even darker and more suffocating, and then the wars of decolonisation spread all over the place. Well, since everyone wanted their independence, let everyone stay at home, there's no point in going to watch other people tearing each other's guts out from close to, the result's always the same, the stench of the abattoir. Henri claims he wants to bear witness. Big deal! The testimonies intermingle, contradict each other, one war follows on the heels of another, eventually you get them mixed up. What's more, victims and killers are often interchangeable. Yes, they can be swapped round, you don't have the good guys and bad guys lined up on either side of a barrier in distinct, fixed groups, all you have in general is people who are basically lukewarm, but who can be fired up or turned cold by circumstances, fairly quickly — and to disastrous effect: it often happens that today's martyr can turn into tomorrow's torturer as soon as the occasion presents itself and yesterday's executioner, having lost his omnipotence and impunity, is bemoaning his fate and screaming injustice. You only have to give human beings full powers and total licence for the majority to start misusing and abusing them without compunction.

Charlam has a very low opinion of his fellow men. He often thinks of the scathing words the Grand Inquisitor, as portrayed by Dostoyevsky, has for the blasted freedom Christ is supposed to have come to reveal and offer to mankind. Although he is obnoxious and cynical, what the old Inquisitor has to say is basically very sensible because it's realistic. He knows that mankind is neither good nor intelligent, that it is composed of a pack of indecisive, fickle and selfish beings. 'You promised the the bread of heaven,' he says to the silent Christ, 'but can it compare with the bread of the earth in the eyes of the weak human race, depraved and ungrateful as they are?' And for this very tangible and consumable bread they envy, exploit and kill each other. Bread — wealth, territory, sex, power, glory: those are the true passions driving the human race, freedom is only a delusion, a sham, a means of satisfying one's desires without constraint.

And then, humans are illogical, once they're free, they get afraid, don't know what to do with this huge gift, it's too much for them, it demands too much effort, especially the effort of thinking, choosing and acting while taking full responsibility for their actions. 'The most constant and tormenting concern of a free man is to find, as quickly as possible, someone to bow down before,' the Inquisitor declares, driving his point home by concluding that, 'even when the gods have disappeared they will still prostrate themselves before idols.' Yes, unlimited freedom is a danger, a poison, dynamite. It is only bearable in small doses and with the ability to manage it. It's like speed, which Georges loved and which killed him because he couldn't keep it under control.

Speed, betting, spending money like water— Georges was a gambler. For a long time Charlam was worried that the vice might resurface in one of the twins, who used to get into fights when they were younger, but no, they've settled down and they're making their way along well-marked tracks and he keeps an eye on those tracks to make sure they're safe.

7

Sabine has never had a dog. As a child she would have loved to have had one but her parents refused on the grounds that a dog was dirty, a nuisance and expensive. They said no to everything. At Hourfeuville there had been cats, household pets and strays coming to see what they could scavenge from the garden, though sometimes the roles were reversed, the domesticated cats wandering off, while some of the vagrants set up home in a corner of the property. Sabine liked their intractable nature, their unpredictable moods and their air of superiority, while dogs were lacking in refinement and, above all, a sense of independence. She had lost any desire to own one.

However, when she goes out at the moment she always has a large black dog at her side, the one Édith had left with her to look after for a couple of days. The couple of days are long since past, they've turned into months already. The day after it arrived, Édith was killed in an accident as violent as the one that cost Georges his life, though certainly more terrible in the last moments, since it took longer before it was over. Her enthusiasm for hang-gliding was to be fatal.

*

The day before the accident, Édith went to see her niece with the dog. Sabine was astonished by her visit, which was both extraordinary and unannounced. There was no contact between the two women, apart from family gatherings, as there was no affinity between them. For the first time Édith had been warm, almost affectionate. They had gone for a walk on the beach, accompanied by Liquorice, who ran along in front of them, barking in his cavernous voice. They talked of this and that, a little about Georges, but as if merely in passing. Then they sat on the terrace of a café, looking out to sea. In the course of the conversation Édith remarked incidentally that she was stuck because she had to go away for a couple of days and didn't know who to ask to look after

Liquorice. Sabine felt obliged to offer. When Édith was about to leave, the dog looked very agitated, so she stroked him and then played at throwing a stick for him again. Very far, skimming across the waves. Liquorice dashed after the decoy and she took the opportunity to slip away. When he arrived back with the stick in his mouth, the dog turned to look in all directions, sniffing on the air the smell of his mistress's sudden disappearance, and he gave a long groan.

That evening Édith watched a performance she had put great care into devising and organising. A few days previously, after numerous nocturnal rounds of the streets, she had approached a prostitute, a young woman with brown hair, and put her request to her: she wanted to watch her making love with a man, also young. She made it clear that she didn't want to take part in the lovemaking, simply to observe it. The girl had reminded her that there were plenty of films, sex shops and even specialised clubs catering for people who got their kicks out of drooling over others having sex, but Édith, ignoring her derisive tone, explained that she wasn't interested in what was on offer to ordinary voyeurs, she wanted a private session, behind closed doors, and nothing fancy. The price she was proposing for this private performance was very persuasive and agreement was reached, it being the girl's task to find a suitable partner.

The woman and her partner were on time for the rendezvous in the hotel where Édith had booked a suite. She had had an enormous bouquet of red and orange roses delivered, champagne and an assortment of snacks. At first sight the demands of their client seemed modest to them and quaint. They were to make love without recourse to very extravagant positions, a nice leisurely little fuck, that was all, and handsomely rewarded. But since they weren't wanted to put on a crude and mechanical pornographic show, what they were being asked to do was more difficult than they had supposed — precisely because they were being asked to make perfect *love*, as if they were in the clasp of a great wave of desire, so gripped by this desire that they were overcome with sweetness. She explained this to them in tones that were both lyrical and impersonal, speaking in a low voice, occasionally falling silent and sketching an uncertain smile or a gesture that remained uncompleted, her hand hanging in the air.

'We're not in a hurry,' she said, 'we have the whole night before us. The whole night, yes… Do not proceed until you feel ready, moved by desire. Take the time to let your desire mount, let it linger within you, languish, stir, quicken… Forget me, forget who you are, forget everything, be — how shall I put it? — innocent. That's it: innocent. As simple as possible. And also make it last a long time. Make love at a leisurely pace.'

Then, turning to the young woman, she added, 'One more thing which is very important for me: go about it quietly, don't speak, don't groan, above all don't cry out. I would like to hear nothing but the man's breathing.'

And, turning to him, she repeated, 'Your breathing. Like a song rising up into the night from all your flesh, from your blood, from your bones.'

She poured some wine into the three glasses and waited patiently.

The man felt ill at ease, he had never been in a situation like this with its mixture of indolence and tension, of delicacy and obscenity, for however much their client might throw around big words like 'love, innocence, sweetness, song of the night tarara-boom-diay…' the fact remained that she was preparing to feast her eyes on him having it off with a tart. He found their client's calmness and courtesy disconcerting, she was confusing the issue, dressing up an ordinary exhibitionist number as something grandiose and chaste. He didn't like this mixture of styles, on the one hand there was work, fucking women or men and pricing his sexual services according to what was asked for and how long the proceedings lasted, and on the other hand there were his love affairs, and they were personal. And then he found the way this refined bawd looked at him disturbing, it was as contradictory as the wishes she expressed, both piercing and absent, determined and vacant. Anyway, he had clearly understood that this farce was all about him, that their client was banking on him, on his body and his breathing, and the woman she'd recruited off the street had acted as bait and now her function was to be a foil to him; he had no doubt that he would be

131

looked at as he'd never been looked at before, into the deepest, most secret recesses of his skin. Far from feeling proud, it made him feel embarrassed and irritated. If there hadn't been a nice lump of dosh thrown in, he'd have upped and left, walked out on the old biddy who was threatening to steal his breath.

The woman was not daunted. She too had guessed that she was playing the supporting role in this story and she didn't care. Their client intrigued her, she sensed a wild passion beneath her placid exterior and also a total lack of experience in matters of sex. Perhaps she was a virgin, an old maid? Without being able to say why, she found the idea amusing and disturbing at the same time. 'Be innocent,' she'd told them. Innocent, them! But it seemed clear that she, the old maid, believed in their innocence, or at least in the possibility of them recovering their lost innocence. And this firm if naive belief surreptitiously became contagious. In fact, the old woman was more of a clairvoyant than a voyeur, a clairvoyant with a screw loose and a kind heart. Right then, she was gong to give this chaste crank her money's worth, she'd have no problem extracting a few groans, both harsh and tender, from her partner in *innocence*. And when, for once, she wasn't being asked to fake an orgasm by giving squeals of sham rapture, shrieks of a woman on heat, she wasn't going to say no.

The woman acted the part so well that she became caught up in it, she felt a degree of sensual pleasure that wasn't normal in her work, perhaps precisely because she hadn't been required to fake a climax with a great to-do, because she had been asked to keep herself in the background. And the man, caught between the body of the girl, astonishingly radiant with silence, and the old woman's ardent gaze — her auditory gaze on the lookout for his breathing — had yielded. Everything inside him had relaxed under the slow surge of pleasure and this pleasure had taken on a rougher, fuller tone than usual as it rubbed against the silence of the woman whose breath was coming in short pants, faster and faster, but always muted.

For a long time Édith contemplated the couple, dozing now, the woman stretched out on her stomach, the man on his back, head to one side and the white sheet pushed down to the bottom of the bed, sculpted into folds which the light from the lamps turned into drifts of ivory yellow. She placed two envelopes full of banknotes on the table, underneath the bouquet, and quietly left.

At home everything was in order. She had spent the preceding days clearing out from top to bottom. Her drawers were empty, not one document, not one notebook, not one letter was lying around. No one could rummage through her affairs, there was nothing left to find. The first thing she threw away was her medical file containing the results of her latest tests, plus the name and address of her doctor, who had told her, at her own insistence, that her life expectancy was no more than a few months. She could always take a course of treatment, but the chances of a cure were faint and the therapy arduous. Since she was condemned, she had decided to take the initiative herself. She had to act quickly, before her strength started to go. Now it was done, her apartment was a mere habitation stripped of all secrets, her dog was provided for and she had paid tribute to the thing she had never tried in practice but had dreamt of all the more intensely, carnal love. The love of a body. Tomorrow she would carry out the last act.

Right to the end she was perfectly calm and clear-headed, scrupulously doing everything her instructor had taught her not to do, making clever use of the winds to drift towards a rising current to be sucked up and, once there, torn apart in the turbulence. Down below, the ground was farther and farther away, unanchored.

Right to the end? Not quite. She was bemused by the violence of the swirling wind, the booming. And there was the lack of air, the intense cold, the physical anguish of suffocation and the pain of the icy embrace. She was seized with animal panic, a cry came to her lips, but she had no more breath, no more voice and even less power of reason, she was no longer capable of thought, she was nothing but a body terror-stricken at the imminence of its annihilation and struggling instinctively, but in vain. The last word, which forced its way, numb with loss, up from the depths of her fear to scrape along the surface of her blue lips was not that of Georges, but: 'Mummy!'

A little girl with a frozen body spiralled down out of the sky like a bundle of blue thistles.

*

Sometimes the dog lifts its head, turns it first one way then another, ears pricked, and freezes for a moment in the alert position. It's waiting, hoping. Then it abandons the hope born of an illusion, drops its head onto its paws and flops down, giving a long sigh.

Sabine didn't have the heart to put the dog in kennels and leave it there for the rest of its life, so she let it stay. At first they kept their distance, strangers sharing the house; she would watch it, slightly worried, not having had any experience of dogs, while it sized her up out of the corner of its eye. They trained each other, little by little. She wanted to put its bed in the kitchen, but that didn't suit the dog at all. It barked in its stentorian voice, sitting right behind the door, until she came to open it, and if she took too long, it increased the volume of its barking, descending to a deep bass. When, in exasperation, she finally came and opened the door, it would stop, nonchalantly tilt its head to one side and wag its tail joyfully, like a metronome setting the beat for a *presto* movement. The cheerfully open way it had of making her look a fool was disconcerting, she hadn't been used to it with the cats, their trickery being less crude. She made a concession, letting it sleep in the sitting-room, but there it cheated her again, stretching out on the sofa, even though she had forbidden it to do so. When she caught it in the act, it would flatten itself on the cushions, ears at half mast, looking at her with the expression of a naive innocent overcome with sacred sorrow, after the fashion of El Greco's Virgins and ecstatic saints. Eventually they came to a compromise, she granted it an armchair.

Liquorice is full of insatiable curiosity, he just has to identify everything with the end of his snout. One day, when Sabine had taken everything out of a cupboard to paint it, the dog weaved his way between the boxes and bags, sniffing them assiduously, lingering by some, ignoring others. From time to time he emitted sighs, rumbling or lapping noises, just to give voice to his impressions. Liquorice comments on everything, even when he's asleep, he's a compulsive soliloquist. Standing on the stepladder, Sabine paid no attention to him, but when she got down, she saw that the dog had torn open a plastic bag containing some clothes, those Pierre was holding in a bundle and had dropped as he dashed down the stairs, the evening he fled. She had kept them as if throwing them away would have meant accepting the fact that he was dead. She had already had to carry out these gestures of submission to an irremediable absence, she had taken part in the process of the obliteration of Georges' body, of the elimination of his physical presence.

The dog settled down in his armchair, guarding his prize, a red pullover, between his paws. He seemed delighted with it, rolling his head over the sweater and giving groans of pleasure. Standing in the doorway, Sabine fixed Liquorice with as look as empty as the pot of paint she was holding. She didn't know whether to be surprised or angry, the beast was definitely more than a burden, it was a disaster. Not content with invading her space, this predator was now eating it up by attacking her possessions. Since he was incorrigible and she felt she had no talent for training, she was going to have to get rid of him. But the dog, entirely absorbed in his simple-minded enjoyment, with no suspicion of having infringed a prohibition, was quivering with joy and also with trust in his substitute mistress. Was she finally going to make up her mind to come and play with him, as the other one used to? He grasped the sweater in his jaws and waved it, shaking his head vigorously while giving stifled yaps, inviting Sabine to a play fight with the woollen rag as the prize. But did she know the rules of the game, which was to pretend any object chosen as a pretext was extremely valuable, to pretend to be aggressive, to exchange grunts and growls, to race, taking care not to catch each other up too quickly, then to throw the object in dispute again with deliberation and verve? She went over to him, still undecided, he thought she had understood and got into position to play, his eyes gleaming with excitement, his body quivering with elation, his tail swishing.

Sabine's anger, although about to boil over, vanished in an instant, basically there was no reason to be angry. The dog was not committing sacrilege by turning a relic into a toy, he was restoring things to their true worth, the said relic was just a piece of old junk that the moths had already dotted with numerous holes. Why shouldn't Liquorice add a few of his own, it would have no effect on Pierre's fate, whether he was dead or still alive. Anyway, he'd never attached great importance to things, getting rid of his clothes when necessary in the same way as animals sloughed their old skin: his Father Christmas outfit, his Gibi costume abandoned in the woods or the clothes he'd worn on that last day jettisoned on the landing. He didn't even open the presents he'd been given. Had he ended up wanting to cut himself off from everything, from the Bérynx family and his life in Hourfeuville which, all things considered, no longer satisfied him, to shed his self in order to try and come out with a new self? Let the dog keep the sweater and make it into his comfort blanket, let him chew the moth-eaten relic to his heart's content.

From that moment on Sabine stopped looking on Liquorice as a burden, even less as a pest, she adopted him. Equally she stopped waiting for news of Pierre, the torment of his disappearance was over. Now it was time to disburden herself by freeing her memory of her obsession with the man whom she had seen as a lightweight when he was present and who had weighed increasingly heavy on her in the course of his absence. With time, absence and presence had merged to be transformed into a vague and soothing feeling. Sabine had come to terms with the elimination of Pierre.

Had the same thing happened to the Flower Girl? Sabine had noticed during her recent trips to Hourfeuville that the bouquet on the trunk of the plane tree, still standing by the side of the road, had not been renewed. An old bunch of flowers there is going black, fossilised inside its dirt-encrusted wrapping. In that, too, the fire of her memory has gone out, or at least died down. The Flower Girl! She must have grown older as well, become forgetful, or resigned, or turned to a new love.

In response to Sabine's change of attitude, the dog decided she was a fit person to take over from Édith; he no longer sticks his muzzle up in the air to sniff for some unlikely trace of the smell of his former mistress.

8

When they realised how much attention she was devoting to the dog, her children made fun of her, telling her she was much more patient and indulgent with the beast than she had been with them when they were young, more affectionate as well. In short, more maternal. She corrected them by choosing a different term: the feeling this dog aroused in her was not maternal but fraternal. Each of the children reacted in their own way to this, René with a dubious pout, Henri by laughing out loud, Marie by immediately dubbing the dog 'Brother Liquorice'. Henri said nothing, not daring to ask his mother the question the adjective at once suggested to him: 'Fraternal like Pierre?' He himself couldn't say whether the question referred to the relationship his mother had had with the man, or concerned the man's character or even the feelings he had eventually had for him.

His two brothers had never concerned themselves much with what had happened to Pierre Zébreuze, his sister and his mother, once the shock of the incomprehensible flight of the Gibi was over, had distanced themselves, the one in separate stages, the other in a gradual drift. What had they lost with that man — a substitute father, a guardian angel, a lover, a friend?

After five 'Zélie' stories, written under the pseudonym of Zoé Zébrynx, Marie, feeling she'd explored all the possibilities of her mischievous little imp, has taken up a new occupation and is working as a stage designer, this time under her real name. For a long time she hoped that Pierre, if he was still alive, would look in a bookshop window and see one of her books displaying the first names of Zoé and Zélie as well as the combination of their two surnames, would understand and get in contact with her again. She knows what she owes him, she knows that she drew a lot of inspiration for her own books from the stories he used to tell her and from the writings of this Zélie she'd found in his bedside table. She opened an account in the name of Pierre

Zébreuze and deposited half of the money she received for the books in it. An account in the name of her co-author, who, however, remains a phantom whose debt is difficult to repay.

Since Pierre did not reappear, she decided to give the money she was keeping for him to an association helping homeless women, like the tramp she saw peeing on the pavement when she was a little girl and who made such an impression on her. A woman in 'aphelion' to use Zélie's expression, kept at a maximum distance from herself and from a world indifferent to her degradation. *'By dint of dying and of being here all the time I have no idea where I am at Even whether I am full stop'* — Marie can hear the soft sputter of these words by Zélie in the drawn expressions of all the down-and-outs she sees as she goes about Paris, stranded here or there, or wandering round aimlessly.

What Henri lost with Pierre is the older brother he never had and that he dreamt of. He never liked the position of eldest that fate gave him and that Charlam emphasised for such a long time after his father's death. He would have liked to have a big brother who would have preceded him, initiated him into games, life, not in the way of adults, who are often hardened, armoured by their experiences, their habits, their prejudices, but as a young man who was close to him and at the same time more mature, more aware. A brother who had gone before him, had scouted out the land. Pierre had started to play that role, when he disappeared.

It is a little because of him that Henri became an itinerant witness, concerned to save from immediate oblivion those hidden lives which pass and fade straight away, engulfed by wars, revolutions; because of that man who will have died without anyone knowing how or why, precisely because there was no witness, and without leaving any traces apart from a large yellow poster, the glow of which is growing dull with time. And yet even after it has lost its freshness, the Rothko remains a window open on the world for Henri, on the unexplored side of the world. There again it is something *hidden*, unperceived, that a man has made an effort to render discernible, perceptible, the hidden side of dramas where the visible and the invisible, light and darkness brush against each other, scratching or caressing each other, where the colours move on the edge of motionlessness in a double movement of contraction and dilation, where a silent adventure is played out in the unknown tract of an expanding space.

'Pictures must be miraculous,' Rothko declared, 'the instant one is completed, the intimacy between the creation and the creator is ended. He is an outsider. The picture must be for him, as for anyone experiencing it later, a revelation, an unexpected and unprecedented resolution of an eternally familiar need.' Henri had this experience and repeated it, he has seen a large number of paintings by Rothko in museums, exhibitions, he has been to Houston, to the chapel the painter decorated with monumental murals, dark pictures in an opaque key of black which he completely drained his strength completing. 'I paint very large pictures precisely because I want to be very intimate and human. To paint a small picture is to place yourself outside your experience, to look upon an experience as a stereopticon view or with a reducing glass. However you paint the larger picture, you are in it. It isn't something you command.'

In February 1970, in the early hours of a freezing morning, Rothko committed suicide in his Manhattan studio. It was true that he was ill, his body worn out, his creativity waning, his solitude increasing, his bitterness even more. Anger and bitterness at the casual way of the world, at the little attention, patience, mediation shown by the majority of admirers of his works, which he had fashioned and erected like temples. But no one, or almost no one, expected him to create temples of oil and canvas to celebrate the mystery of colour, the vibrations of light, the power of the dark diffusing a subtle luminosity which was both harsh and delicate. In the eyes of other people, his large canvases had eventually acquired more commercial than spiritual value, and that cut him to the quick.

Suffering from being a 'stranger' to his finished pictures, which no longer needed his presence, did he go to find himself again in the intimacy of his paintings, did he leave to meet himself in that unknown realm that he sensed pulsating endlessly in the colours, from the most limpid and solar to the darkest? Leave to find himself in order the better to relinquish himself, unless it was the opposite, that he abandoned himself in order to be finally brought face to face with himself. In death, inside and outside are inverted and embedded, and 'It isn't something you command,' even if you bring it about yourself by cutting your veins.

To an admirer who was sensitive to the contemplative force expressed in his paintings and who thought that he must be a 'mystic', Rothko replied, 'I'm not a mystic. A prophet perhaps — but I don't prophesy woes to come. I just paint the woes already here.' In his matter-of-fact way, Rothko had put things back in their place: not a mystic, an overworked word, a prophet if you like, but one who didn't claim to predict the future, who had no pronouncements, neither blazing nor hazy, to make, a prophet who restricted himself to saying what *is* because he made the effort and had the patience to look. To look to the point of hearing, to listen to the point of seeing the light shining through things, to the point of discerning residues of night dispersed through the day, traces of bare light in the darkness.

Henri also observes, he says and shows what is happening in the world, not as a painter slowly extracting his vision from the limbo of the canvas set up in his studio, but as a photojournalist always on the move, on the lookout. Modest and persistent, he brings back pictures, he is a prophet of the present, of emergency. But sometimes he becomes weary and wavers. He has seen too many horrors, too many murders committed without qualms, without remorse, too many deaths without consolation. Wars have scoured the rose-tinted film from his eyes, scraped to the bone the beliefs and ideas he had gradually built up since childhood, starting with his belief in God and trust in his fellow men. They have blurred his reference points, dismantled the frontiers between good and evil, intelligence and stupidity, instinct and reason, humans and animals. From now on he's not surprised at anything, at what anyone does, himself included, usually the worst, sometimes a noble act.

War, that ancient mistress with the ever young, shining eyes, the look of La Pasionaria heroically defending her country, liberty, the people, her view of man or her idea of God etc.; the look of Medusa mesmerising men so as to incite them to hack each other to pieces; of a Bawd forcing women and little girls into prostitution; of a Madonna weeping for her children, tortured, mutilated, burnt alive, their throats cut, disembowelled, shot, blown apart... Her children of all ages, from old people to babes in arms, sometimes even infants who haven't been born yet torn from their mother's guts, for a laugh or as a preventive measure. Does he hate it as much as he thinks, as much as he would like, this huge hydra that is war? Could he have acquired a taste for it, out of a mixture of repugnance, fascination and weariness? Acquired a taste for these extreme situations, these wild scenes where the same proceedings are repeated ad infinitum, the same non-dialogues consisting of cries of rage, sobs and supplications, death rattles and sharp silences. Acquired a taste for these scenes of chaos, of hectic cruelty studded here and there with a few kind gestures, a few shattering looks of simple humanity, incongruous, disconcerting details which you have to learn to seize in the middle of the tumult. To do what with them, when all's said and done? A little salt to season his journalistic prose, touching anecdotes to reassure himself after all about human nature?

The more Henri questions himself about his status of 'witness', the more he's plagued with doubt. How can he be sure that what he is recording is truly faithful to the facts, enlightening? However impartial he is determined to remain, there are always choices he makes, consciously or not, and however alert he is, there are always events which, happening beyond his field of vision, escape his notice. There are so many blind spots: in the towns in revolt, on the battlefields, in all areas and inside himself. Henri places the most dangerous of these blind spots in the brain, somewhere in one of the folds, and in that hiding place is a beast, insomniac though appearing to sleep, a sort of cranial 'Sleeping Fury' ready to pounce at the first opportunity.

The brain. He once performed a sketch about it with his brothers, his cousins and Pierre Zébreuze in the garden at Hourfeuville. He can't remember what he said, but it must have been a long way away from reality, naive as he and his fellow performers still were. His pontificating as a mad professor was inspired by the Shadoks, failed birds with wings as stunted as their brains, but he didn't mention the insect Jenny, a nasty little beast more venomous than all the Shadoks put together and supposedly the first and sole inhabitant of planet Earth before the arrival of other creatures, which it welcomed with a flame-thrower. Jenny, the diminutive of the slightly old-fashioned Christian name 'Jennifer', or the abbreviation for 'portable generating set' widely used during the war in Algeria? Ridicule and vileness, Jenny was a good mixture of the two. It would be the right name for the archaic beast lurking in the depths of the human brain which comes to life when a war, a revolution, a disaster occurs.

But Henri does not allow this basically banal conclusion, which overwhelms him on certain days, to lead to the disillusionment with and contempt for the human race in the manner of Charlam, whose views and arguments have a musty smell of old wines that have gone stale and vinegary from having been left too long in the cellars. He realises that there are other blind spots in the minds of men, other neglected, unrecognised areas and much more remarkable ones at that. There is no Jenny in them, nothing stamping and raging, just a silent sigh, the glimmer of a dream waiting to unfurl, patience ever dawning. And all of that living together in the same semidarkness, consigned to the same ignorance. And Henri tries to take *all of that* into account, but only just manages to do so, that, too, is not something you command. That is why he constantly returns to the areas where men are in conflict, to go to meet them, speak with them, try to understand despite everything.

9

For eight years Pierre, alias Jesus the Bullock, kept silent. At first it came from a complete inability to speak or think, so great was the stupor resulting from the dislocation of his mind caused by the gob of spit. His mental life seemed to have put itself on hold, only maintaining the functions that were strictly necessary to keep the bodily machine going. But this state of suspension did not last as long as his behaviour led others to believe, it lasted until new connections had been established in his brain on the ruins of the old ones. Then he ventured into labyrinths even Doctor Zagueboum had not discovered, not even suspected. This exploration demanded as much calm and concentration as discretion. He therefore went to great pains to observe the injunction Zélie violently rejected: to behave oneself, keep quiet and toe the line. His docility was neither forced nor faked, it was just the expression of complete indifference to himself as much as to everything around him. He was constantly sleeping, when standing up as well as lying down, sitting, eating, walking, washing himself, eyes open or closed. He slept incognito, assiduously.

In his apparent somnambulism he was in fact engaged in continual, intense activity: he was breathing life back into his memory, sharpening his awareness, polishing his lucidity, his judgment, scraping the deposit off his heart. He was working at his release, at setting his mind free. He travelled the paths of dream in acute sleep mode. He practised without respite the art of the animal they had made his totem out of their inability to find his true name and also out of derision: he ruminated.

He ruminated and he plodded along, slowly, deliberately, digging over his mind, opening up wide furrows with various remains, gnarled roots, relics gleaming at the bottom. He broke through the sediment of oblivion, of anxiety, of shame that had accumulated and hardened inside him, he turned over the sticky, shapeless mass crawling with all his ills. He was exhuming himself. And the man who was unburying himself was neither alone nor whole, he appeared in sections tangled up with other bodies, of which three, wild parasites, both devoured and nourished him.

The body of his mother, the body of his father, the body of his little sister.

The naked body of his mother
  the wasted body of his father
    the fallen body of his little sister

The body of laughter, the body of fear, the body of excess

  in a void of laughter
  in the dread of fear
in an effusion of silence

Yet on her wedding day young Céleste Bergance was wearing a very pretty dress. Taking short steps, she walked up the aisle on her father's arm, her black eyes shining with jubilation and pride. When they arrived at the altar, her father stood to one side as she waited, upright and lustrous from head to toe, for her bridegroom, led by his mother, Jeanne Zébreuze, to join her by the chairs upholstered in red velvet that were reserved for them. And the ceremony had begun with its hymns, its readings, the soaring peals of the organ and the homily from the priest. The grand ritual of the nuptial mass proceeded in perfect harmony, Céleste was in tune with the atmosphere and with her Christian name. But the countdown to disillusionment was approaching zero. At the moment of the exchange of rings, to an outpouring of sound from the organ and amid the fragrance of the bouquets of flowers and the incense, the bridegroom, on the point of becoming her husband, leant down and whispered in her ear — so softly that the priest and the altar boys couldn't hear, clearly enough for the woman concerned to understand every word — a murderous little statement, 'I don't love you, Céleste, and I don't think I ever will.' He said it in a detached, slightly weary tone. Céleste would not have felt such a sharp, burning pain had a hornet plunged into her ear to drive its sting into her eardrum. Her hand clenched just at the moment when Pacôme was slipping the wedding ring on her finger and he had to force it down, dislocating one of the joints. The combined effect of the sudden letdown and the pain in her ringed finger, made Céleste burst out in a fit of laughter. The priest, who had blessed any number of marriages since he had been in charge of the parish and had never seen a maiden express such joy on her wedding day, was very moved. He concluded that the love that united this couple must be deep-rooted and would bear fine fruit.

Having entered the church radiant on her father's arm, Céleste left it shaking with laughter on the very uncertain arm of her husband. She stumbled back down the aisle, her head and shoulders jerking convulsively, one fist pressed to her mouth, one finger battered and bruised, to the perplexed looks of the congregation. Pacôme, for his part, affected a vacant air.

He wasn't malicious, just a frustrated man and of a character so indecisive as to be weak, which often produces the same effects as malice. It never occurred to him that to declare his non-love to his bride, who was very much in love, at the precise moment of the exchange of rings, was offensive and cynical. He had done it in response to a sudden need for openness; a belated need, but no less sincere and urgent. For a while his admission assuaged his conscience.

It wasn't that he felt any animosity towards Céleste, in fact he quite liked her, but he wasn't in love with her at all. Nor with any other woman either. It was an emotion that was foreign to him, women had never attracted him in that way. He enjoyed their company, the strength and wit that were peculiar to them, he could admire their beauty, their elegance, their imagination, when they had any, but they aroused no desire in him. Their friendship was enough. Only men attracted him. During adolescence his first feelings of love had been aroused by boys of his own age, which had left him distressed and confused. At seventeen these feelings had focused and blossomed in a passion for one of his school-friends but, too fainthearted to act on it, to declare himself, he had turned in on himself and put all his energy into denying this attraction, which was generally seen as an affront to nature, to society, to morality, to God, and consequently condemned without appeal. Despite this, his parents had eventually come to suspect his scandalous leanings, without ever discussing it openly between them, perhaps even without admitting it to themselves, and as the years passed they worked with increasing feverishness to get their son to marry. Now the deed was done, they were relieved, honour was saved, what happened next was nothing to do with them, that was Céleste's problem.

The curse of laughing until it hurt, until she was exhausted, had come to stay. The fits erupted every time she suffered a disappointment or an affront. It happened when she lost her virginity, which was also when Pacôme lost his. She was so mortified by his clumsiness and the repugnance he showed that she laughed so much her body ached and she was short of breath for hours on end. Nevertheless a child was conceived following another trial of sexual congress. When he learnt his wife was pregnant, Pacôme decided he had fulfilled his conjugal duty and from then on spared himself the torment of these wheezing exertions. Eventually they had separate bedrooms and Céleste became accustomed to a life of semi-solitude between a husband who was seldom there and a child that was putting on weight in her stomach. She welcomed her pregnancy as an amnesty authorising her to resume her place in common reality, in normality, and the laughing sickness went away. But she had a relapse the day after her child was born. Once again it was Pacôme who triggered off the fit when he told her he had registered the child under the name of Éphrem and not that of Pierre as she wanted. Éphrem! Where had he dug up a Christian name like that, where, if not from one of his male loves? Once more she felt betrayed, scorned, reduced to a mere instrument, and she broke into a long burst of monotone laughter. The infant at her breast started to cry, the milk flowing into its mouth was tasteless and its mother's face aslant above it was contorted in a horrible grimace. They had to take the child away from her. It was several hours before she calmed down, exhausted. From that day on she was unable to breast-feed the child and it was handed over to a wet-nurse.

She refused to call her son by the official Christian name Pacôme had imposed on him, sticking to her own choice of Pierre. But the shadow of Éphrem, the great love of her husband's youth, the more long-lasting for never having been consummated, fell between her and the child, creating a distance she never managed to break down. She was hard on him, regarding him as a bastard who had surreptitiously slipped inside her in order to take on life at her expense. He didn't look like her at all and so much like her husband — and perhaps like the other man, who knows! How can one be sure that impossible loves do not avenge themselves by obscure magic tricks? She treated him harshly, often made fun of him, but sometimes she softened, the child was gentle and loved her unreservedly. He lived just for those moments when his mother relented, forgetting her misfortune and her anger, and held him tight, made a fuss of him at last, moments as intense as they were rare. Patience and affection came from his father, who neither looked for nor suspected any particular resemblance, to have a child was enough for him, a source of wonder; but Pacôme kept that wonder hidden and almost the only mark of his affection was the name he called his son when they were alone together, and even then he spoke it in a low voice: Éphrem.

Pacôme had made a tree-house for his son in a lime in the garden, a tree-house such as he would so much liked to have had himself when he was a little boy. A hut perched among the branches where he could be alone with his dreams, his questions, his torments, well away from adults. He gave Éphrem this wooden hermitage that he himself had lacked.

One day the boy asked his mother why she never called him Éphrem as his father did. All he got in reply was a slap. He didn't dare ask any more questions about that, not of his father any more than of his mother, he just accepted it as another of the adults' peculiar ways. For one of them, the name of Éphrem meant the sweetness of a smile, a caress, for the other, the violence of a slap across the face. He played along with this game of split personality, being now Pierre, now Éphrem, he wanted to be liked by both his parents and did his best to be the hyphen joining them. But the two names remained separate, as painfully separate as the two people who each stuck to the one or the other. In his hut between heaven and earth, he would repeat to himself, 'I'm called Pierre-Éphrem, I'm called Pierre-Éphrem,' in a low voice, for himself, for all three of them. For no one. His secret incantations were swallowed up in the rustling of the leaves, the buzzing of the insects, in the tracery of birdsong, the creaking of wood and the whistling of the wind.

The discordant aspect of his name fell abruptly silent when his father left. War had come, settling in the defeated country like an imperious guest, a guest that needed servants and slaves, and gathered together a large number. Pacôme was one of them and was sent to work in Germany. The child felt crippled, having lost his father and Éphrem. Now, up in his refuge, it was his father he called, 'Papa, Papa…', he tried to ward off war, absence, his own fear. Gradually his mother became less irascible, gave him more of her time, even a little kindness, to which Pierre responded with a joy that was both intense and ambiguous: his mother's love came at a price: his father's exile and the banishment of Éphrem.

Céleste was more surprised than anyone at the change in her feelings towards Pacôme. Far from rejoicing at his removal, which looked as if it was going to last indefinitely, she was annoyed, worried about it. She knew his health was delicate and he was an odd character, solitary, how would he withstand this enforced expatriation, captivity in all but name, the ordeal of hard labour and of the lack of privacy, the separation from his son? She wished him no ill, there had been enough of that at work in both their lives, ever since the violent exchange of rings, and that was their affair, nothing to do with others. If there was to be ill, then at least they should suffer it together, here, under the same roof, together and separated, united and apart, united in disaster.

With Pacôme gone, their son was no longer a challenge, a wound, the visible shadow of a rival in love, he was just a lost child. She therefore showed him more care and attention than in the past, not because in that way she could make him her own — she still regarded Pierre-Éphrem as a child conceived outside of her, a foreign body maliciously deposited in hers but with no roots in her flesh, no true bond with her, as if he were the son of Pierre and Éphrem — but because through him she could show Pacôme a little of the love he had devastated with a word and which persisted despite that.

There was another surprise in store for her, this one a cause for jubilation. She met a man with whom she found once more the joys of love and finally discovered the sweetness of shared pleasure. What she was discovering was quite simply physical love, as if, despite the birth of a child, she had remained a virgin. But her lover was called Johann Böhmland and wore the uniform of the enemy. So what? It was a long time since things had run smooth in Céleste's life; had her husband, in his wedding outfit, not thrust a declaration of non-love, of definitive non-desire at her? Why should a man in the outfit of the occupying forces not make her an opposite declaration. They balanced each other out. Pacôme had been allocated to Johann's country, Johann assigned to Pacôme's, the one was loath to go near her, to touch her, the other was in love and attentive, the one was taciturn, the other cheerful and warmhearted. She was disarmed by this cheerfulness, which until then had lost its appeal, its meaning for her. To her Johann was not a soldier, one of the occupying forces, but simply a man full of vitality, humour, sensuality. While remaining discreet, she did not attempt to hide her liaison with him and when she became pregnant, she bore it with a serenity she had not felt during her previous pregnancy. This child was not an alien graft planted in her body, reducing it to an instrument, but truly a bud of her flesh, opening out and growing in her womb.

She often laughed, but now it was a normal laugh that rang out short and clear. Pierre would listen, wavering between unease and rapture, at the new laugh his mother was continually spreading round the house, the yard, the garden. She seemed more beautiful than ever, so much nicer than formerly, even though harsh, sometimes crude comments about her whistled past his ears in the school playground or the local shops. The price to be paid for the happiness that had finally come to the house thanks to the change in his mother as she grew more and more radiant and affectionate was increasing: his father's disappearance and, outside, the mockery, insults, sidelong glances and lips pursed in disgust or commiseration.

A little girl was born to whom Céleste gave the Christian name of her maternal grandmother who had died a few years previously, Zélie. This choice led to her final rejection by her family: the newborn child, marked by a double stigma — illegitimacy and dishonour to the nation — was not worthy to inherit the name of a forebear who had been respected and loved by all. But Céleste stuck to her guns, she had left behind the state of submission to the order imposed by those around her, obedience to the tacit law of the proprieties, feeding on so many lies, myths, gorging itself on suffering, resentment, latent madness. Showing the boldness Pacôme had lacked, she refused to accept the duty to put on a front dictated by the tyranny of the conventions and the fear of what people will say. She bore no grudge against the man who was forbidden to follow his inclination in love, who was forced into a role that he was unwilling and unable to fulfil, now she was sorry for him. She decided that the time of sabotage and evasion in love was over, she gave back to her son the part of his name she had refused him, Éphrem, thus recognising and accepting the indirect paternity of her son and by that relieving them both of a weight that had been attached to this hidden tie for too long.

But Céleste had overestimated her bravery and independence or, rather, underestimated the strength of the resentment towards outcasts and moral bankrupts, she never imagined how unyielding the hatred could be among those who, not having taken any risks during the war, contenting themselves with keeping their heads down to ensure their survival, hate themselves for their pusillanimity, feel humiliated and, when all danger is past, take it out on a men or woman who had the effrontery to snap their fingers at the war, fear, appearances. A very convenient scapegoat. After the Liberation Céleste was labelled as such and treated accordingly.

Circus animals are paraded decked out in absurd, tawdry finery: pompons and plumes, chains and little bells, brocade waistcoats or brightly coloured capes, little boaters or pointed hats. Conversely, fallen women are exhibited divested of all their finery, starting with their natural adornment, their hair, especially if it is long and beautiful; sometimes they are even stripped completely bare.

A naked woman, her head shaven, put on show in broad daylight in the streets of a town or village for the delectation of a fully clothed crowd of people, all neatly brushed and combed, wearing hats and, above all, their dignity on a ribbon round their necks — such a woman will walk in ungainly fashion, without the least elegance. Céleste submitted to the shearing without a word, even though it was carried out brutally. She refused to get undressed so some of those dispensing justice did it for her, tearing off her clothes. What modesty could she claim, a slut like her who showed no hesitation in stripping off for a Hun and having it away with him while her husband was slaving his guts out in Germany? It was too late for modesty, she no longer had the right, let her show everyone the 'truth' of her body, of what she was: a cesspool dressed up in a pretty skin. Go on, don't let her fool you any longer, you can see through that deceptive skin, it's just the wrapping for cheap flesh, common meat for the soldiers, a belly for the enemy to fuck, for any kind of vile obscenity. And didn't she have a brat with her Fritz, well, let them parade together, the tart and her Kraut girl. And they stuck Zélie, thirteen months old, in Céleste's arms.

She stumbled along, head bowed, back bent and her knees stuck together, her arms round Zélie clinging to her neck. She had fallen into a lower state than submission, she had sunk to one of servility, of a brutalised puppet.

A man stepped out of the jeering crowd that was following her and started to conduct the chorus of furies, brandishing his walking stick and breaking into the *Marseillaise*: '*Allons z'enfants de la patri—e—: le jour de gloire est arrivé!*' It triggered off a fine, very uplifting effect as the chorus took up the majestic strains of the song and the national anthem rang out in vibrant tones. Carried away by this choral ardour, the leader of the choristers started to tap Céleste's head and shoulders with his stick, sublimated into a conductor's baton. He didn't hit her hard, he wasn't trying to hurt her, he was just beating time. It was a solemn moment, justice was being done, an affront was being avenged, the harlot, the unfaithful wife, the mother of a bastard girl, was being punished. '*Aux armes, citoyens! Formez vos bataillons! Marchons, marchons!*' And suddenly she started to laugh. As on the day of her marriage, as when her son was born, only a louder, longer, more resounding laugh. What she produced was a kind of whinny, shrill and syncopated, making her double up even more, and she continued on her way, screwed up in a Z shape like an exhausted thunderbolt, her spine and shoulders shaking with wild laughter. Zélie, panicking at the din all around and, above all, at the strident noise in her mother's chest, right against her ear, started to struggle and cry. The choir was sliding into cacophony as it begged the sacred love of their country to guide, to uphold their avenging arms… '*Liberté! Liberté chérie… Allons z'enfants…*' pom-pom, pom-pom on her head and back, braying laughter and bawling tears, as the choir assured themselves that Victory would come running at their manly strains… '*Marchons, marchons!…*' rat-a-tat pom-pom.

Her other child, her son, consigned to the care of a neighbour for the occasion, heard this commotion. Eventually he distinguished his mother's laugh and his little sister's crying at the heart of the uproar. His mother's sick, demented laughter, the way she used to laugh, and Zélie's crying, now like the screech of a saw. He ran out of the house and towards the commotion. *Allons z'enfants* the day of shame has arrived, the great day of obscenity! He saw his mother, pale from head to toe, all hunched up under the angry cries, the jets of spittle coming from all sides and, huddled in her arms, Zélie, whose nappy had come loose and was dangling down under her bottom. Indignant voices could be heard in the crowd: 'It's a disgrace! A disgrace!' without it being clear whether the exclamation was aimed at Céleste as a whore who had gone over to the enemy or as a woman who was being humiliated, or even expressing disapproval of the use of the patriotic song, entirely out of place in this farce of justice. 'What are you doing here?' a woman exclaimed when she saw the son of the shaven-headed victim. 'This isn't the place for you. Off you go!' When Pierre-Éphrem didn't move, she grabbed the sleeve of his jacket and dragged him away. Another woman shouted that enough was enough and several voices joined in to insist that it was time to stop hounding the woman. When she got back home, Céleste continued to laugh to the point of fainting.

When, some weeks later, Pacôme came back, he found Céleste cooped up in the house with the shutters closed. She was wearing a scarf wound like a turban round her head, accentuating the deeps lines on her face, which seemed sharper. Her eyes were hard, as if mineralised. She stood up when he came in, but said nothing, just stayed standing there in front of him, her arms hanging down slack. Putting the bag he had over his shoulder on the floor, he went up to her, very slowly. When they were face to face, he smiled at her and murmured, 'I know... ,' adding, 'There's no need to be afraid,' and raising his hands towards her turbaned head. She took a step back but he, without abandoning his gentleness and determination, undid the scarf. She gave a groan and stiffened, he placed one hand over her mouth to silence at source any harmful laugh that might take hold of her and said, "Don't laugh, Céleste. You don't need to be ashamed. You're beautiful, even like that.' It was a new beauty he saw in her, harder and purer.

But she wasn't ashamed, she didn't feel unworthy before her own conscience, for she had no regrets about having loved and having lived out that love without pretence, openly, with an honest heart. She hadn't harmed anyone. To caress a man's body, to kiss him, to unite with him in the intimacy of a bedroom, away from the war, was not at all a crime. It was something else that hurt her. She could not forget nor pardon the humiliation which had been imposed on that love through her, the rejection, the denial and the profanation of that love by a community that knew nothing about it and did not want to know. And she declared, 'I am not ashamed. I hate them. I hate them for everything they've done to us.' Pacôme understood, from her tone and the expression in her eyes, that the 'us' included him, that it did not refer to her and her illegitimate child alone, but that it also applied to the ill-suited — unmatched even — pair that they had formed, and in the same moment he understood, from the solidarity of that 'us', that Céleste had forgiven him all the sorrows and disappointments he had inflicted on her since the first day of their marriage, through weakness, cowardice, thoughtlessness. She had given him absolution. She was so much stronger than him, refusing to submit, to resign herself to lies and hypocrisy. She had had the courage to live out something he had not dared to try: to love according to her choice, to follow the thrust of her own desire. And she had gone through with it, to the point of giving birth to a child. He admired her.

Pierre-Éphrem didn't admire his mother at all any more, at one stroke he had lost all trust in and respect for her, all that was left were scraps of feeling, tattered love. He had seen her naked, naked in public, naked and befouled. He had seen her reeling like a drunk and bald like an infant or an old man, like a convict. He had seen her wailing, pitiful, degraded and passing the horrible canker on to his little sister by direct contagion. The sight had been so violent, so ugly, that from now on he could only see her in that light. The image of his mother, defiled, grotesque and nauseating, kept superimposing itself, disturbing his vision of his mother's body, however well dressed it was, and of her face, however washed and made up it was, after she appeared to have returned to normality. He could not stop himself feeling revulsion towards her, and also rancour. These feelings were confused but persistent. He felt she had betrayed him, not because for a while she had replaced his father with that German soldier and had another child — Pierre-Éphrem loved his little sister and hadn't disliked Johann, the soldier devoid of any martial conviction, a generous, jolly man who had brought cheerfulness to the house — but because she had not been able to escape from those insane puppeteers who had made her revert to the state of a cow, a bitch, because she had let herself be hounded through the streets in broad daylight, in front of all the people. And, what's more, with his little sister. Two blinded bodies, blinding in their nakedness, two bodies covered in a dull whiteness gleaming with spittle. Two bodies, one large, one miniature, repulsive in their nakedness. Two ugly puppets driven this way and that through the streets, the one emitting deranged laughter, the other screeching like a saw, against the background of a throng crowing the *Marseillaise.*

They left the town where victory was celebrated with insults and vengeance meted out to a few women guilty of ordinary love affairs made out to be high treason, and settled in another town where no one knew them. There Pacôme found work as a keeper in a zoo and once Zélie was old enough to go to school, Céleste went to work there as well, as a cashier. Even more than the change of place, it was the company of the animals that brought the couple relief that was both sweet and ambiguous.

Sitting all day in her wooden hut with its half-moon-shaped window, Céleste listened to the cries and laughter of the children mingling with the calls of the animals. She liked all this noise, the hubbub of human and animal voices, and yet she often felt a dull pang at the sound of the happy children looking at the cages of the captive animals.

In the morning or the evening, when the zoo wasn't open yet or had closed for the day, she would take a turn round the walkways with a silent greeting for all the occupants of the enclosures and cages. She knew the name of every one of them. She sniffed all the strong smells, some pungent, heady, others almost sickly sweet. She sought eye-contact with the wolves, the big cats and the Arctic foxes as well as with the antelopes, the lamas, the ostriches with their huge obsidian eyes, or with the wild oxen and the does, the owls, the monkeys or the peacocks. She was looking for a sign in their eyes, a reproach, an appeal, an expression of revolt or of entreaty, but their impenetrable looks slid across her as if she were a pane of glass; beautiful looks, with a shimmer of confused dreams, haunting nostalgia for other latitudes, other climates, and also crazed looks, simmering with boredom.

She always finished her round at the little enclosure for the tortoises, Fantine, Babou and Ginette. With them there were no looks to track, no fury or distress or blame to detect, just astonishment to probe. The oldest, the most colossal of the three, was called Fantine, she was well over a hundred and weighed almost six hundredweight. She had an immense stillness that was fascinating, she was a mass of patience, a block of life in slow motion, even dormant. Perhaps she did not belong entirely to the order of living creatures, but stood at the junction of animal, vegetable and mineral? Her shell recalled a bronze shield, plates of pinkish brown schist, or a tree stump hewn into a rounded, dented shape, her head and tail were similar, like horny truncated limbs, and her huge crooked feet looked like cracked leather sheaths intended to hold anything from pebbles, weapons, gold coins to nuts or statuettes. Céleste wondered what sensations were felt by this archaic animal with a weight of years as heavy as that of her body, her stomach almost always pressed to the ground. Had the weight of time deposited in her flesh, solidified in her skin, given rise to a memory, to an inkling of consciousness?

Pacôme never talked about the years he'd spent in Germany. When he came back his health was impaired, his lungs were affected. He was thin, moved and walked slowly — an emaciated, coughing tortoise. He showed Zélie the same attention and affection as he did to his son, he had adopted her right away. But he insisted they should be open about this adoption, the time of things unsaid, of lies was over. When Zélie was old enough to understand, he explained that he wasn't her natural father, that her birth was due to another man, that he was a second, legal, foster father. That had caused a certain confusion in the little girl's mind. Two papas, a natural and an artificial one, a true and a false one? But why, then, had the false one been declared legal? Did that mean that the true one was illegal, an outlaw like Robin Hood? Since all this seemed to proceed according to some bizarre logic with absurd inversions, could it be that her true father, the outlaw, was as horrible as her false father was nice? The questions she asked her big brother, who had been fortunate enough to know this odd, contradictory father, came up against a harsh refusal. 'Can't remember a thing,' he claimed. 'Stop pestering me with these stupid questions. Why don't you go and ask your mother. If anyone knows anything, it's her, not me.' But although Céleste didn't respond to her daughter's questioning with a point-blank refusal like Pierre-Éphrem, she was evasive, it hurt to evoke the memory of the man she had loved.

Johann had disappeared as he had come into her life, following the fortunes of war. Had he managed to return home, safe and sound? If so, why had he not written? Had he forgotten, even renounced her — her and their daughter? It was true that their move had been done in haste and discreetly. It was up to her to find him, but she didn't know how to go about it. All she had to go on was a handful of names: Johann Böhmland, living in the vicinity of Cottbus in Saxony, a region which, being behind the Iron Curtain, was now cut off, inaccessible. She didn't even have a photo of Johann, there was nothing, only the child, this lively little girl, forever asking questions and given to moods. She could be jubilant one moment, sad the next, chattering excitedly then abruptly sulking, as nice as pie then a raging fury. She sometimes had bizarre ideas, such as feeding the birds of prey, the golden pheasants and the pink flamingos with words. She wasn't interested in the tortoises at all, they were far too lifeless and silent — and ugly too! She couldn't understand the affection her mother felt for them, these ossified old dames clearly didn't feel anything at all, her mother was wasting her energy for nothing. The birds now, they were something different, all lightness, speed and, some of them, an explosion of colour. And above all they produced sounds, cries and songs. The point of throwing them regular handfuls of words, freshly gathered from the dictionary or learnt in school that morning, was to enrich their cries and songs with vitamins. What she was really feeding by this kind of thing was her own imagination, always on the alert, on the move, an imagination fired from the outset by the admission of a reality that was too vast and complicated for her to grasp, to assimilate, to come to terms with. They had told her too much and too little, just enough to arouse her curiosity about her 'true' father, magnified by the mystery surrounding him, by his status as an outlaw, his position as a notable absence and a familiar stranger. She had asked Pacôme what the German for father was, since that was the man's mother tongue. She had asked for the word for *father*, not for *papa*, that was reserved for Pacôme, who performed the function perfectly. *Vater. Mein Vater. Mein richtiger Vater, Herr*

Johann Böhmland. Mein Vaterland. His sole function was to exist somewhere or other, untouchable, invisible, living behind a 'curtain of iron', a long scar cutting Europe in two from what she'd seen on a map in her brother's geography book.

When she was thirteen, Zélie ran away. She was found three days later, wandering near the German border. She wanted to get all this clear in her mind, finally put a face and a body to the name of Johann Böhmland, to ascertain whether her rounded lids and periwinkle-blue eyes really did come from him, as her mother claimed. Given this resemblance, she did not doubt that they would recognise each other as soon as they came face to face, but to make even more sure, to emphasise the supposed resemblance, she had cut her hair very short, like a boy's. She wanted to make herself into a miniature Johann Böhmland.

During the three days she was away, Céleste was like the animals in the zoo ceaselessly pacing round and round in the restricted space of their cages, an animal, her eyes crazy with confinement, burning with worry, lack of sleep. When the runaway was brought home, exhausted and, above all, mortified at having failed in her venture, she stood before her mother, upright and silent, her little face hard with anger. And for a moment Céleste thought she was seeing herself as she had been forced to appear twelve years ago. Time suddenly contracted inside her, her eyes were filled with with a swirl of images, her ears with a turbulence of noises, cries, her stomach with a dull wash of laughter. Her child was back, saved, alive. Yes, but saved from what and alive with what kind of life?

Her child… *'Allons z'enfants de la patri—e—, le jour de gloire est arrivé!'* The *Marseillaise* rose up in her stomach, rose like a stagnant pool suddenly forced up out of its hole, slimy with mud, with moss, sticky with viscous laughter and sobbing hiccoughs. *'Allons z'enfants…* Come children, children of my handsome loves, children of my shat-upon loves…' Her son, her daughter, so deeply marked by the imprint of imagined fathers that it made her head swim. And myself, Céleste, who am I and what is my place in my children's songs, eh? And where am I in those of the men, in the hearts of the two I have loved? Oh, and you my parents, my two brothers and my sister and you, the friends of my childhood who all stayed down there in the town where I was born, turning your backs on me, tell me, what is left of me in you? Just a whiff of sadness and disgust, already distant and fading more with every day? Come children, come my men, come my parents, my friends, make an effort, look at me. Look at me, for Christ's sake! To arms, form your battalions! March on, march on...

And the glutinous singing poured out in a gurgle of laughter and crushed words over the much-impaired tune of the *Marseillaise*. But, unlike previous times, this outburst of laughter, with a tattered song clinging onto it, was not loud, was not strident. It came in fits and starts, interminable sobs in ugly modulation. Pacôme tried to hold her tight to calm her down but she elbowed her way out of his embrace. No, no, not the touch of a body, no more body, too late, she wanted to be left alone in her frantic laughter, alone in her unconstrained song, alone in her convulsive weeping. And she ran this way and that, throwing her arms about to avoid being seized, no one should come near her, no one touch her. She twisted and turned, zigzagged as she ran, her shoulders jerking with spasms, like a medicine-man in a trance, a shaman conferring out loud with the spirits of the earth, the rocks and the waters, with the spirits of fire, of the wind, of the dead. 'March on, march on, *z'enfants*, march as one, tiddly-pom, tiddly-pom...' The spasms spread progressively to all her muscles and organs, and she remained in their grip until her heart, exhausted by the torrent of constrictions, gave way.

It was Zélie who had the idea: Céleste should be buried in the tortoise enclosure, not surrounded by anonymous graves in a cemetery. Her mother, she thought, had suffered enough from her fellows, including her own daughter, Zélie, so they shouldn't insist she remained in close proximity to humankind for the rest of eternity. Céleste had felt a special affection for the tortoises, especially for big Fantine. And who knows, perhaps it was the spirit of that placid colossus her mother had been invoking in her yelping, shuddering witch's dance? Hey, hey, Fantine, come and chew up all my days, my unhappy loves, like lettuce leaves, like grass, like a clump of nettles, come and swallow me mouthful by mouthful down into your old stomach and let me decompose there, slowly, come and sit on my untombed corpse, softly, softly, to hatch it like an egg taking a long time to ripen, with a view to a new birth.

The burial took place one night. They had broken the seals on the coffin where Céleste's body had been put, after having been duly examined on the day she died. Pacôme filled it with the same weight of sacks containing soil and stones and it was that sham coffin that was taken to the cemetery the next day. Zélie had suggested the idea of the substitution, Pacôme and his son had carried it out, the first removing the body of the dead woman, the second digging a narrow trench in the tortoise enclosure during the night. And once the trench with its secret was filled, they planted a honeysuckle over it.

The fatal consequences of her flight and pathetic return had sobered Zélie up; she abandoned the idea of going to look for her father again. She no longer had any desire to meet this unknown man who — at a distance, it is true, and entirely ignorant of his responsibility — was involved in the death of her mother. What would she have to say to him, now, as an introduction? — 'Because of you my mother died singing out of tune, bent double with laughter and hiccoughs,' or perhaps, 'You've been left the widower of another man's wife, of your wartime amour in France. Did you really love her, by the way?' She turned to her foster father, her false father who was so much more real than the true one, and she started to address him by the formal *vous,* which he and her mother had always used to each other. This gave him a new dignity, she was finally according him the title of 'father' in addition to his quality of 'papa'.

But Pacôme was no longer in a state to exercise any authority at all, his health was deteriorating, soon he had to give up work. Tuberculosis was diagnosed and he was sent to a sanatorium. Zélie was fourteen and a half and there was only her brother, who had just come of age, left to look after her. Pierre-Éphrem, who was in the third year of his course at university, gave up his studies to find work as quickly as possible, the casual work he'd been doing in his free time wasn't enough any more. He changed jobs several times, in every one of them he was bored, felt out of place. But he was even more uncomfortable in his role as guardian, especially since Zélie, who now made him the object of her affections, which were both restless and exclusive, was unpredictable, completely unamenable to discipline, to a sense of moderation. When their father died, one year after going to the sanatorium, Zélie's emotional instability grew worse. On the pretext that she couldn't stand idiots, she would let anyone feel the rough edge of her tongue, in the street, in the shops, at school, where she was twice suspended for insolence and insubordination. She had no friends. Whilst her phenomenal cheek, the liberties she took, commanded the admiration of some of her classmates, it also frightened them and left her isolated. Although her teachers recognised her remarkable intellectual maturity, they would not tolerate her sudden changes of mood and her impudence.

Following a further scene, not serious in itself but one further item on a list that was already deemed too long, Pierre-Éphrem was summoned and advised to take her to a psychiatric institution for consultation as a matter of urgency. Exasperated by the constant worries Zélie was causing him and above all afraid that the laughing sickness that had caused her mother's death might reappear in her in one form or another, he complied. It took a great deal of patience and cunning to persuade his sister, who was suspicious of all institutions, to go to the hospital with him. He assured her the visit did not commit her to anything and swore that she would not stay there, not even for a single day. She believed him, he was the only person she trusted.

She did stay there, and for more than a day. In all she stayed for three hundred and ninety-one. Not once during that long year did she agree to see her brother. One afternoon, taking advantage of a momentary lapse of attention on the part of the staff, she went into a room that had no bars on the window, opened it and threw herself out, ending the number of her days three floors below. Tomorrow would not be another day, tomorrow would no longer be the punishment increased by an empty today, tomorrow, finally, would not happen, Zélie had gone Elsewhere, to a great nowhere, an 'expanding Globus', her hair tangled up with spaghetti in tomato sauce.

*

Jesus the Bullock has gone back in time, often stopping on the way to examine this or that moment of his involute past, spending a long time stroking its calluses and spiral knots until he wears them down, disentangling, dishevelling them in the stellar wind. Through this painstaking task of untying and polishing he has gradually said good-bye to his ghosts, set his terrors, his regrets, his grudges free. Given absolution to his departed loved ones.

Thus he descended by meandering degrees to the night of his conception, a sad night foundering in his mother's laugh of shame and distress, an echo to his father's panic. He revisited the limbo where the hazardous encounter between two minute cells laden with stories, saturated with rumours and marks, took place and illuminated them, brought peace to them.

In the clear light of this appeasement, of profound detachment, he brought himself back into the world in reverse. He turned round the obscure workings of the forces which had him in their grip, which exercised a hold over him, by going on further, well upstream of the limbo, as far as the thin but surging source of life, a limpid, fiery flower, the scent of which, both fleeting and intense, dazzled him. Now the living person is no longer vested with the inheritance of the dead, being weighed down, hampered by it, it is the living person who has embraced the dead, unburdened them, extricated them from their ills. Now let each one go in liberty, light as a bird. Let Zélie be free of all laws of gravity to fly on the cosmic winds, the luminous winds of this Elsewhere she dreamt of behind the bars of her room.

The body of his mother

The body of his father

The body of his sister

Little constellation of extinguished stars of flesh, returned to dust, but whose ardour was such that it continues to radiate long after their extinction.

Mouth relieved of its clots of laughter
Desire freed from its shame
Words in their Sunday best

The body of her son of her brother

Release

And Marie, what had happened to her, to her brothers? And Sabine?

Pierre-Éphrem straightens up in silence behind the impassible mask of the Bullock and, without making a sound, gathers the forces he has drawn in the course of his long internal journey, concentrates them, gets them ready. He has reached the end of his period of latency, of apparent lethargy, his moult is complete, he can leave. But he shows nothing of his revolution, of the transmutation of his fears into boldness, of his shame into peace of mind, of his weaknesses into energy, of his desires into willpower. He does not want to delay, he does not want to have to explain himself. You can't explain the smell and the incandescence of a windflower.

He makes surreptitious preparations for his departure and slips away one night so nimbly he's gone before anyone notices. Jesus the Bullock, the harmless idiot, the sleepwalking mute, has disappeared into thin air. Pierre Zébreuze has defrocked himself once more. This time it's for good.

He's gone back to square one. But this square one is not a hole, not a void nor destitution, it's a beautiful ring in the water of time, ready to open out and swell up, a globe of fire easy to pick up, a ball. Pierre runs away.

He no longer runs at random till he's out of breath, nor does he let himself be buffeted by a damp, dreary wind, as he was before, he walks with sure steps. He goes to Hourfeuville.

The Summerhouse

It's nothing, I went away from myself
the way forests go to the night
edged with wild roses to silence
the heart rending.

Jean Grosjean

The summerhouse stands in the middle of the garden, it's made of wood carved like an Arabic latticework screen. A tangle of ivy and honeysuckle makes a cupola in a variety of shades of green from a dark green that's almost black to a delicate pistachio or almond; according to the season and the time of day, it can take on a bronze, bluish, golden or absinthe tinge.

On this late-summer afternoon its shade is heavy with fragrances, quivering and rustling with the light wind, the buzzing of the bees. It is round and full, like a breast. In this globe of warmth, of greenery, of honeyed odours, Charlam is sipping a glass of cool tea. Of very black tea, spiced with a few drops of lemon juice, which give it a dark-red sheen. He dissolves lump after lump of sugar in a little spoon held on the surface of his drink. When the square of white sugar has been transformed into a rounded, ochre oval, he raises the spoon to his lips and sucks up the contents. 'How many grains will there be there in that lump of sugar?' he wonders as he savours the mouthful. 'As many as there have been days in my life? Fewer? More?'

He closes his eyes and dozes for a while. Like the sugar lump moistened by the tea, his memory dissolves, similarly breaking up into tiny grains — scraps of images, sensations, memories. All this residue is very old, the present rarely appears in his dreams, on the other hand it occupies his mind all the time when he's awake. He has lost none of his haughty pride, on the contrary, the older he gets, the more he blossoms. He wears his eighty-three years lightly, he has no serious or disabling illness, his mental faculties are intact and the cane he does need to help him walk only enhances his patriarchal air. A twisted walking stick in fawn-coloured wood with an amber knob that his grandsons gave him for his eightieth birthday. A sceptre symbolising his octogenarian status. He gave himself a fine present the previous year, he got married again. It's not good to grow old alone, a companion at one's side is a support, reinforcement against the dangers of the twilight years. The woman he chose is as sound in health as in her affections and her judgment.

He wakes with a start, pestered by some insect buzzing close to his ear. He drives it away with an irritated flap of the hand, a gesture that is in tune with the brief dream that was disturbing his sleep. He was dreaming of Édith and he found that unpleasant. Every time the memory of his sister appears in his mind, he needs to get rid of it as quickly as possible, before it can gain weight and establish itself in his thoughts, so tiresome does he find it to be reminded of her. If she hadn't insisted on being a daredevil, throwing herself headfirst into activities unsuitable for her age, she would still be there among them. She had been as stubborn in exposing herself to danger as she had been previously in protecting herself from the outside world and noise. To kill yourself gliding, how stupid could you get! He thumps the ground with his stick. If it wasn't enough for him to lose his son then his first wife. But he misses Édith more than Andrée; even when she used to shut herself away in her apartment with those voiceless mutts, she had a presence that was more dense than that of his wife. It was because she was a Bérynx, despite everything, and then she had largely been brought up by him, in a way Édith was his first child, his little sister/eldest daughter… Grasping his stick in his fist, he hits the ground again to halt his memory, which is threatening to switch to full flow. Keeping hurtful memories at a distance, muzzling wearisome thoughts, that is his defence, his mental hygiene, one of the keys to his longevity, together with the virtues of married life.

He pours himself another glass of tea and opens his newspaper at the crossword, something on which he is very keen. He returns to a clue that has been causing him problems, a long word of thirteen letters, the last down clue on the right-hand side. All he's got are a few consonants, an *r*, a *c* and an *n*, he hasn't managed to get a single vowel and he still can't work out the clue: 'Car scene bores when mixed up in complex ramifications.' He concentrates on the across clues, hoping the end letters will allow him to solve the stubborn clue. 'Sets traps', in seven letters. Poacher, of course. The word reminds him of something disagreeable, but he can't remember exactly what. The vague memory fades as quickly as it came, leaving no more trace than the faint circles that insects sketch on the surface of a pool when they briefly touch it in their zigzag flight. Good, that's another *r*. And the next: 'Loses colour', five letters. 'Fades', really easy. That gives him an *s*, which is not much use as it's at the end so must indicate a plural. Still no vowels, so no progress made.

A football whizzes into the summerhouse, hits the inside edge of the roof and bounces back onto Charlam's knees, where it comes to a stop. A woman's voice tells the clumsy kids off for almost having hit the old man, but he throws the ball back to them from the summerhouse and the children disappear with shrill screams. How many great-grandchildren has he got already? He starts counting again, as he did a while ago when trying to work out the number of his days and of grains in a lump of sugar. Eleven? Twelve? Most of them come from the Fosquan side, Madeleine's sons have large families, Georges' are much less prolific, only the twins have produced any children. The fact that Marie hasn't got any children doesn't bother him, but Henri… Oh, Henri, a constant disappointment and cause of worry to him. Irritated, he shakes his head, to clear it of that source of vexation, just as he sweeps everything that upsets him under the carpet, and returns to his newspaper. 'Pavilion', eleven letters. Initially he sets off down the wrong road, looking for words meaning 'flag, banner, standard', but then changes his mind and comes up with the word that fits: 'summerhouse', which finally gives him a vowel. As he writes in the letters, he tells himself that he prefers 'arbour' or 'bower', they're much more elegant, but even if Hector and his wife insist on calling it a summerhouse, it was still an excellent idea to build one here in the middle of the garden; Hector can enjoy the calm on the days when the restaurant is closed. 'Ceremonial dress', four letters … The bell at the garden gate rings. 'I'll get it, I'll get it,' Charlotte shouts as she rushes off to the gate. 'The restaurant's closed today and don't open to anyone you don't know,' Charlam calls out after her. 'Of course, I know that.' She continues to run, she likes seeing new people, listening to strangers asking questions through the bars of the gate and then acting as messenger.

There's a tall fellow standing at the gate. He greets her and smiles. She thinks he has a very beautiful smile and his eyes are a strange colour, silvery grey, as if bathed in moonlight. When he asks if Madame Bérynx is there, she nods and gallops off to the house. She's all out of breath when she gets there and says, 'There's a man at the gate who wants to speak to you. He's got eyes like, like…'

'Well? Like What?' The little girl has forgotten, but another image comes to the rescue: 'Like puddles of rain with sunlight in them.'

'He's not going to bring any rain, I hope?'

'Of course not, since they're full of sunlight!' She shrugs her shoulders at this lack of common sense in an adult then rushes off to play with the others.

The visitor watches the woman coming down the tree-lined drive. She's quite plump, her hair is grey, almost white, the whiteness accentuating her fresh, delicate complexion. When she reaches the gate, he greets her with her name: 'Louma.' She takes a step backwards to get a better look at this stranger who has addressed her in such familiar fashion. She frowns, thinks and hesitates, while he looks at her in astonishment. It's true that his eyes are a sparkling grey, Charlotte was right. 'Louma…', he says again. And suddenly she exclaims, but in a hushed voice, 'Pierre!' She takes another step backwards, not to get a better look at him this time, but instinctively, to keep herself at a distance. She has stiffened, with her arms hanging down, fists clenched, and has difficulty breathing. 'Yes, it's me —' She doesn't let him go on. 'Who me? What me? No, don't say anything, I don't want to hear it, but you're going to listen to me. It's too late to reappear like this, it's too late to come back, there's no place for you among us any more. No place for ghosts from the past.'

She speaks in a low, halting voice, her jaws set, her shoulders and fists too, staring at him out of large, round eyes blazing with surprise and fury, but above all with anger. He makes one more attempt: 'Louma…' She goes up to the gate, grasps the bars and, her face pressed against the ornamental ironwork, continues her diatribe: 'Shut up! You've no right to speak any more. We had people searching for you, we waited for you for years. Then we stopped. We thought you were dead. And by appearing to be dead, you ended up by dying as far as we're concerned.

What did you imagine we'd do? Treat you like the prodigal son and kill the fatted calf? We've better things to do than that. Life went on without you, and it will go on without you. Don't come and upset our lives again. Go away.'

She lets go of the gate and backs away again. He hasn't moved, he looks at her calmly and his calm makes her impatient to see him clear off. 'If it's Sabine or one of the children you're looking for, you're wasting your time. Sabine left Hourfeuville several years ago and made a new life elsewhere. Marie's not here any more either and she's doing fine at the moment. I don't think they would want to see you, you've caused them too much pain. Go away, I tell you, it's best for all of us. What have you to offer them apart from futile regrets, dissatisfaction? You'd stir up discord in the whole family, you're nothing but a purveyor of illusions and, anyway, you're the one who reduced yourself to the status of a ghost. Go back to the limbo you came from and don't come here again.' But he remains motionless, regarding her without showing any particular reaction, neither resentment nor annoyance, neither protest nor resignation. And that is what Louma cannot stand, his sovereign, radiant serenity.

Yes, Charlotte was right, the 'man at the gate' does have eyes the colour of sunlit rain, the colour of wind. Their luminosity is fierce, immediately transfixing anyone exposed to it. A look that lays bare and probes, scours and questions. But how far might this acuity of vision take one, towards what abysses, what dizzying precipices, what inner revolt? Louma does not want to take this risk, neither for herself, nor for her loved ones, she has worked hard for so many years to preserve a modicum of well-being in this family and she has finally received the reward for her devotion, she has obtained recognition and security and she has no intention of relinquishing what she has for an uncertain gain. In fact is there anything to be gained at all?

'Never!' she declares in her muted voice. She turns away abruptly and goes back up the drive. She can feel Pierre's eyes on her back for a few moments, then nothing. She slows down, she can't stop herself glancing back. There's no one at the gate. Pierre has left.

She has a musty taste in her mouth, as if she'd been chewing mouldy bread, and her hands and feet are so cold she could well believe it was winter.

Charlam has left the summerhouse to settle in a deckchair in the sun. He is having his siesta, the newspaper spread as a sunshield over his face. Louma pours herself a glass of tea with lots of lemon to get rid of the taste of mould on her tongue. It's so sharp it makes her screw up her eyes. She sees the pages of the newspaper flutter in the breeze, it looks like an old grey bird having trouble taking off. One page then another detaches itself and slides down to the ground. She goes to gather them, carefully removes the rest of the newspaper before all the pages slip off, and in its place puts a white handkerchief over the face of her husband, who hasn't woken up. Then she goes back to the house to make the children's tea. As she pours the stewed peaches into their bowls, she keeps silently repeating to herself, 'No place for ghosts from the past.' It's just the same whether they're dead or not; if Georges, Andrée or Édith were to reappear, she'd have done the same as she did to Pierre, she'd speak roughly to them and send them packing, however painful it might be to do so. Everyone in their place, that's the price of peace. She puts a shortbread biscuit in the middle of each bowl. The peaches give off an exquisite fragrance.

Pierre walks slowly away. He is unaffected by the scathing reception, he is no longer in a hurry, on the run, no longer full of shame and anxiety. Of course he isn't a prodigal son, he isn't a son and he hasn't been through a prodigal's experiences, nor has he a prodigal's desires since he feels neither the remorse nor the destitution. He has not come to Hourfeuville to beg anything, he simply wanted to celebrate his deliverance, to greet those he knew and loved. He will find them, one day or another. He descended into the dark labyrinths of his memory and stayed there a long time in order to go and meet his dead and make his peace with them, he can equally well venture into the maze of the present to search for the living so that he can renew acquaintance with them.

He stops for a moment, his face to the wind, which bears so many smells. He breathes in the peppery, slightly sweet odour from the bushes on the embankment. There is a silkiness to the air, the sun is already low on the horizon, the hour of its setting is approaching. It seems huge, both powerful and light. It has an intense yellow glow and spreads broad streams of orange across the sky. '*Globus! What do men know of the night? They only enter it as intruders...*' And the day, what do they know of that? What do we know of the light? Pierre wonders at this outpouring of sparkling yellow, the prelude to twilight. A long, slightly undulating streak of white crosses the saffron immensity.

Pierre is upright facing this sky of incandescent radiance; he can inhale its brilliance, its breath, its space. He is inside it. To be *inside,* 'it isn't something you command,' as Rothko said. It is something that is decided in the depths of one's being, a will asserting itself with the force of the obvious, of love, a resolution suddenly imposing itself from having spent a long time ripening in the darkness. Pierre is inside this flood of light which is soon going to topple over and surge back, he is in the flow of time, at the heart of time. He is standing in the embrasure of a tremendous picture undergoing boundless expansion and variation, in the splendour of the visible. He is in the dazzling nakedness of desire, at the core of life itself.

A football hits him on the shoulder. He turns round but cannot see anyone on the road. All he can make out is a slight movement in the branches of a lime tree overhanging the wall round the Bérynx house which he is still quite near. He picks up the ball and goes back. Through the foliage of the lime tree he sees fragments of a child: a rounded knee, smooth and shining in the sun, a hand clutching a branch, the faded blue of a pair of shorts and the steel-blue, accentuated by white stripes, of a T-shirt; above the apricot skin of the knee are two shining eyes. It's the little girl he saw a while ago at the gate. She's watching him attentively. Holding the ball in his hands, he smiles at her, his head back, leaning to one side. He starts juggling with the ball, slowly at first, then quicker and quicker until finally he throws it over the wall. The girl stands up on the branch where she was squatting in order to follow the trajectory of the ball which flies in a steep curve over the trees before falling into the garden. Pierre hears her laugh, a few fluty, resonant notes, like the song of a reed-warbler.

Recommended Reading

If you enjoyed reading *Hidden Lives* there are other books by Sylvie Germain which might appeal to you:

The Book of Nights
Night of Amber
Days of Anger
Medusa Child
Prague Noir: The Weeping Woman on the Streets of Prague
Infinite Possibilities
Invitation to a Journey
The Book of Tobias
The Song of False Lovers
Magnus

If you have enjoyed the emotional intensity and gritty realism that characterise parts of *Hidden Lives* we recommend the following books:

Zero Train –Yuri Buida
Prussian Bride – Yuri Buida
Pleading Guilty- Paul Genney

If you like books with stories within stories and literary game-playing we recommend the following books:

Music, in a Foreign Language – Andrew Crumey
Pfitz – Andrew Crumey
D'Alembert's Principle –Andrew Crumey
Satan Wants Me – Robert Irwin
Exquisite Corpse – Robert Irwin
The Arabian Nightmare – Robert Irwin
Mr Dick or The Tenth Book – Jean Pierre Ohl
Lucio's Confession – Mario de Sa-Carneiro
A Box of Dreams – David Madsen
The Double Life of Daniel Glick – Maurice Caldera

These books can be bought from your local bookshop or online from amazon.co.uk or direct from Dedalus, either online or by post. Please write to **Cash Sales, Dedalus Limited, 24-26, St Judith's Lane, Sawtry, Cambs, PE28 5XE**. For further details of the Dedalus list please visit our website at www.dedalusbooks.com or write to us for a catalogue.

The Book of Nights – **Sylvie Germain**

"*The Book of Nights* is a masterpiece. Germain is endowed with extraordinary narrative and descriptive abilities ... She excels in portraits of emotional intensity and the gritty realism of raw emotions gives the novel its unique power."
Ziauddin Sardar in The Independent

"The novel tells the story of the Peniel family in the desolate wetlands of Flanders, across which the German invaders pour three times — 1870, 1914 and 1940 — in less than a century. It is hard to avoid thinking of *A Hundred Years of Solitude* but the comparison does no disservice to Germain's novel, so powerful is it. A brilliant book, excellently translated."
Mike Petty in The Literary Review

"This is a lyrical attempt to blend magic realism with *la France profonde*, the desolate peasant regions that remain mired in myth and folklore. Nothing is too grotesque for Germain's eldritch imagination: batrachian women, loving werewolves, necklaces of tears and corpses that metamorphose into dolls all combine to produce a visionary fusion of the pagan and the mystical."
Elizabeth Young's Books of the Year Selection in The New Statesman

" ... a lithe, magical-realist account of how the primordial woods of northern Europe were overwhelmed by the twentieth century both tremulous and shocking."
James Saynor in The Observer

£8.99   ISBN 9781873982006   278p   B. Format

Night of Amber – **Sylvie Germain**

Night of Amber ranges from the terror and atrocity of the Algerian War, the Paris of the 1960s and an unforgettable evocation of la France profonde with a host of memorable characters. It is a powerful and emotional novel, which takes *The Book of Nights* to its dramatic conclusion.

"There is little that can be said that would do justice to the controlled brilliance of Sylvie Germain's writings – *Night of Amber* is a fantastic book, a wildly inventive novel about childhood, death, war and much else. It creates a rich fantasy world, yet it is also very moving, and deals with the emotions of grief and love with an understanding and insight which few writers can match."

Edward Platt in *The Sunday Times*

"Germain's sequel to her prize-winning first novel, *The Book of Nights*, follows her anti-hero Charles-Victor Peniel on his hate-filled journey through life. It sings with a strange poetry, pitting politics (the Algerian war and May '68) against the vagaries of individual minds."

Ian Critchley in *The Daily Telegraph*

"Sylvie Germain is arguably the greatest writer of her generation."

Meridian Book Programme, BBC World Service

£8.99   ISBN 9781873892952   339p   B.Format

Magnus – **Sylvie Germain**

Winner of The Goncourt Lyceens Prize and shortlisted for The Oxford Weidenfeld Translation Prize and The American Library Association Notable Book Awards.

"Sylvie Germain's melancholy, magical tale is told not in chapters, but in tiny 'fragments', the first two of which are missing, interspersed with poems and shards of prose that resonate throughout the text. It's a chamber piece, a life compressed, sometimes waywardly mystical, in places furiously erotic, and never less than fascinating in its take on history, memory and the Holocaust. Christine Donougher's poetic prose suggests an uncanny meld of author and translator; and Dedalus demonstrates again its constant capacity to surprise."

Shaun Whiteside in *The Independent*

"Close to the end of the Second World War, a young boy afflicted with memory loss flees Nazi Germany with his mother and father. A teddy bear named Magnus is the boy's only tangible possession, the one item linking him to moments he can no longer remember. After his father vanishes and his mother becomes mentally unstable, the boy is sent to live with relatives in England. While at university, he journeys to Mexico, where he uncovers a dark secret from his family's past, propelling him thereafter to take the alias Magnus. As he continues a life journey that spans continents and years, this restless, inquiring soul matures, learns, and loves, all the while yearning to unravel the mystery of his true self. Magnus' story is told through "fragments," "notes," and "resonances," which gradually piece together the nonlinear periods of his life. Award-winning French writer Germain's vibrant narrative is interspersed with poetry by Paul Celan and Shakespeare and slices of prose by Juan Rulfo, which makes for a mystical and passionate mosaic of identity, myth, and memory."

Leah Strauss in *Booklist*

£9.99   ISBN 978 1 903517 62 8   196p   B. Format